Monday's New Beginning

Janice Hildreth

Ricki,
Happy reading!
Janice Hildreth

Monday's New Beginning

ISBN 978-1500736033

Cover: Brian Cox

Author photo: Jana Waddell

This book is dedicated to

Mike's and my best work:

Jana, David, Jennifer

Chapter 1

Chloe Evans paused in the playroom doorway and saw the future of her prosperous day care business a hairs breadth away from bouncing into the red. With the super-human reach she had perfected over the past four months, she snatched the scissors from Daniel's hands a mere second before Marissa's French braid became history.

"Daniel!" she shrieked. The small male wearing Harry Potter eyeglasses cocked his head inquiringly toward her. She stopped and readjusted the volume to her *inside* voice, "Daniel, you are never to use scissors. Where did you find these?"

Always willing to own up to his culpability, Daniel readily explained, "Miss Chloe, you used them this morning to take the tag off Zach's new shoes, 'member? I saw you put them in your desk drawer." Rushing to head off her frown, he offered virtuously, "You said we are never to touch anything on your desk, but it was in the drawer, not on the desk."

She closed her eyes, "Daniel, you are never to touch anything on my desk or in my desk, ever. Do you understand?"

Wilting under her stern gaze, he nodded, solemn as a judge, "I guess prob'ly Marissa's mama doesn't want her hair cut, or she would do it herself, huh?"

She couldn't help herself. She reached down and hugged him, breathing in his little-boy scent and finding comfort in the warmth of his sturdy form, "Yes, we'll let Marissa's mama cut her hair when she wants it cut." She gave him a light swat on the seat of his trousers and sent him on his way just as she heard someone pull into the driveway.

Deke Hudson slid his vintage blue and white, 1964 Chevy pickup to a stop in front of the house and turned off the ignition. He was at least five minutes early, so he paused to savor the view. *Begin as you mean to go on* was his motto, and he was sure that showing up early would only make this new boss expect it. Therefore, he wasn't going to ring the doorbell until *exactly* eight a.m.

He turned his head to study the Victorian mansion, which was elevated above the street in the manner of many homes in Seattle. Probably built at the turn of the century, it had been meticulously cared for and was a pleasurable sight to someone who appreciates architecture. The house was painted slate blue, with highlights of cream and deep burgundy. A driveway led from the street, alongside the house, and disappearing around the back. The property was a graceful accent to the upscale neighborhood, and sitting on a Queen Anne side street, it afforded a panoramic view of the Seattle skyline and Elliott Bay. Although he'd lived here for almost a decade, he never tired of the city's beauty.

His beeping watch signaled that it was straight up eight o'clock and reminded him there was a mini-tyrant waiting inside. He grabbed his clipboard and swung out of the cab. At the top of the steps he thumbed the doorbell and waited. The discreet brass plate beside the bell acknowledged that this was *The Perfect Child Bi-Lingual Daycare*.

Immediately the door swung open, and she stood there, still (as far as he could tell) in a snit, "Well, at least you're on time."

He eyed her warily and answered her greeting,

"Mrs. Evans." His memory hadn't failed him. As far as he was concerned she was an extremely attractive woman. She was tiny and very feminine, dressed in black tights, a short black and green plaid skirt, and a dark green sweater. The green in the sweater reflected her deep, emerald eyes. Her copper hair appeared to have been cut with a weed whacker; it was all different lengths and sticking out at odd angles from her head. It looked gorgeous on her, but coupled with her manner, the resemblance to a hedgehog was astounding—little and prickly.

Chloe eyed him on the doorstep and thought dismally, *Nope, it wasn't a fluke*. And she had so hoped it had been. A week ago he'd come to bid on her remodel and turned her world upside down. She remembered the physical shift she had felt the moment she opened her door and looked into his dark brown eyes. And after shaking his hand she had to restrain herself from pressing her fingers to her lips, the tingle was so pronounced. Shaken by her emotional response to him, she had hoped his bid would be too high or he would be too busy. No such luck. Not only had his bid been reasonable, he had been the only one who was available to begin immediately. She had been forced to hire him for the job. Well, just because he was a hunk didn't mean she had to act like a love-sick adolescent.

"Come in," her tone was resigned.

Deke stepped over the threshold and stopped in silent admiration. Before entering a few days ago, he would have bet his Harley that this home had been ruined. He had winced, contemplating the damage from little fingers banging toys on oak wainscoting and tricycles ramming into baseboards. It has been a pleasant surprise to discover that The Perfect Child co-existed harmoniously with the house.

At approximately five thousand square feet, the home boasted two staircases, an honest-to-goodness library and parlor with original oak sliding doors, and six bedrooms on the second floor. Because the damage was minimal, he wondered if her clients' income was a factor. Maybe the wealthy *were* different, and their kids were taught from infancy to respect beautiful things. Maybe, but he didn't think so. He was just pleased that the rooms remained beautiful.

Before he could speak, they were interrupted, "Miss Chloe?"

He turned to observe the chubby tyke tugging at her skirt. If Deke had ever seen anyone who should be wearing a sign that said *Kick Me*, it was this kid. He was dressed in miniature wing tips, dress slacks, an oxford shirt, and a cardigan. Small, round, wire-rimmed glasses completed the nerd image. Deke barely suppressed a shudder at what awaited this mini-CEO in real life.

The youngster persisted, "Who is this?"

She smiled down at him, "Daniel, where are you supposed to be?"

Shocked, Deke turned to make sure the sweet response to the little rug-rat was actually coming from her mouth. Amazingly, it was.

Daniel pointed, "In there."

The sound of feet hurtling down the stairs complemented the distraction. In tandem, all three turned toward the door in the hallway. A moment later someone evidently grabbed the doorknob, because the half in the hallway fell off and hit the floor with a clang. A heavy hand banged on the panel, and a voice yelled, "Hey, Mom!" Immediately the door popped open from the force, and a young teen entered the room. As he passed

Daniel, he handed him the remnants of the knob from his side of the door, "Nice work, Danny. Hang onto this, and I'll show you how to reattach it when I get home from school."

Daniel beamed up at his teen-aged hero. "'Kay, Zach, I was pretty good, huh?"

"Yeah, buddy, but maybe Mom, I mean, Miss Chloe, didn't want the doorknob off. You know?" Daniel looked perplexed at such an inexplicable viewpoint.

Chloe grabbed Daniel's wrist and stood to watch her darling (although currently non-communicative son) morph into Adolescent Brat Boy. He'd completed this transformation every morning since they had moved to Seattle. She stretched up to kiss his cheek and he almost fell into Deke trying evading it. A moment later he was out the door and off the steps.

"Sorry," she tried to smile, embarrassed that Deke had observed Zach's brush off. "I should remember thirteen-year-old boys don't care for mom's kisses."

He gave a nice smile that crinkled his eyes, "Or at least not when anyone else is around."

His kindness almost brought her to tears, and she wondered again why this was happening. Being attracted to a man at first sight was just plain silly. She didn't know anything about Deke Hudson. He could be married for all she knew. The absence of a wedding band (okay shoot her, she'd looked) meant nothing; a ring was dangerous on a job site. *Besides, your relationship with God is the only thing that has kept you sane the past year and a half, so falling for someone on the basis of physical attraction is only asking for heartache.*

Beside her, Deke observed the juvie headed down the hill, attired in a black duster with top-of-the-line sneakers on his feet. The morning breeze caressed a purple Mohawk and glinted on the multiple piercings on his face. Deke braced himself against the familiar rush of pain and then reconsidered, *Being childless means no teenagers*. Maybe there was an upside to not having a son. If his son had lived, he would be about the age of this kid, and he'd probably be the parent showering adoring looks on him. What *was* the matter with her eyesight? If he were a betting man, he'd wager the little delinquent gave her a lot more problems than refusing to allow her to kiss him goodbye.

His eyes shifted to the woman beside him. The sadness in her expression made his heart clench. Her head lifted, and for a moment they gazed at each other without defenses. He saw her pain buried beneath the brisk façade, and she glimpsed his haunting sadness.

But the moment was shattered as Daniel wriggled in her grasp like a worm on a hook, trying to make a bid for freedom. Deke quickly stepped back so she could shut the front door. With escape circumvented, she concentrated on the small one, leaning so she and the chubby toddler were eye to eye, "Daniel, Miss Chloe needs to talk with this man, please go sit by the other kids and watch the video with Miss Maria until Miss Chloe comes right back."

Lost in bemusement over her sweetness with the tyke, she was already through the dayroom before Deke snapped to and followed. Good thing his legs were long because she could really cover ground. And walking obviously didn't overtax her lungs, because she didn't pause for a breath, "Okay, I unloaded everything from the porch yesterday after work."

He was surprised, and his expression showed it, "I thought moving the furniture and equipment was part of my contract."

She scowled, "I know, but the more I thought about you only working four days a week, I realized if Zach and I did this, you'd be that much farther ahead this morning."

He winced recalling her incendiary reaction to his work schedule. If he remembered correctly, her voice had reached a register only accessed by dogs. He suppressed the urge to apologize again, saying mildly, "Can't imagine why it has you in such a flap. I'm still working a forty to sixty-hour week; I'm just doing it in four days instead of five." No way was he giving up the one day a week he concentrated on his dream. If his growing orders kept at their current pace, he would be able to quit the remodeling business and build furniture full-time within a year.

"Yes, but think how far along you'd be if you worked ten to twelve hour days five days a week, or six days a week." Her face brightened as sudden inspiration hit her, "If you'd work six twelve-hour days, you'd finish in almost half the time, and then you could take a full week or two off." She felt brilliant. *That's good, he'd be gone that much sooner and no longer a distraction.*

He frowned, "I'd be dead; that's what I'd be. And why not seven days as long as you're pushing?"

"Oh, don't be such a wuss," her look was scornful. "I wouldn't ask anyone to work on Sunday."

"Uh-huh." He felt amusement warring within him. He was going to have his work cut out to keep pace with her. He kind of looked forward to it; it promised to be entertaining. "It wouldn't matter if you did ask. I'd never work on the Lord's Day."

They reached the kitchen, and she disabled the alarm that sounded when the door opened. She unlocked the door, allowing him access to the fenced backyard.

Since his first chore would be to remove the fence, rendering the kids' playground inaccessible for almost a month, he hoped the door alarm was enough to deter young Daniel.

Chloe watched Deke head through the gate. She turned away, refusing to watch his tall, strong frame as he disappeared around the corner of the house. She didn't have time to stand around.

She headed to the classroom and stuck her head inside the door to check up. Maria was leading the children in counting to one hundred. She was bobbing her head and marching along, while a line of preschoolers followed her like ducklings, bobbing their heads too. As soon as they counted to one hundred in English, they would reverse the direction of their march and count again in Spanish.

She grinned; anything Maria did was done with gusto and grace. The kids loved her. A curvy, middle-aged, beautiful Latina, she had been married to Jorge for thirty-five years. They had four gorgeous adult children and were the devoted Mama and Papa to twelve grandchildren.

At her interview when asked why she would like the job, she had leaned forward to share, "My Jorge hit the roof when Consuela had our twelfth grandchild." She had deepened her voice to mimic her spouse, "'You're going to send us to the poorhouse, woman! Get a job and spend your own money on the grandkids!'" She had eased back in her chair and said with satisfaction, "So that's what I'm going to do. Now when he comes home and don't find his supper on the table, he will think twice about what he said to me." Her cheerful manner, not to mention her fluent Spanish, was exactly what Chloe was looking for in a co-worker, and she had hired her immediately.

The idea for a bi-lingual day care in Seattle came from the experience she and Phillip had when they enrolled Zach in one in California. Chloe learned Spanish during her childhood in Southeastern Washington where the orchards provided work for a growing population of Hispanic day laborers. Phillip had spoken three languages, Spanish being one of them. They had both believed that a second language was important for a child, and research showed that children fluent in two languages were ahead of their peers in problem solving and other skills. A bi-lingual school targeting the significant Norwegian or Japanese populations of the Northwest may have made more sense, but you had to go with your strengths, and Spanish was hers.

She crossed the hall to the music room where Mrs. Thompson, her second full-time employee, was overseeing a group watching Sesame Street. Of all the adults at The Perfect Child, Mrs. Thompson had the advantage of knowing what she was doing, because she had owned her own preschool before retiring. She found retirement boring and was happy to hire on with Chloe. Her manner was brisk; she wasn't the one the children ran to with *owies*—that was Maria or Chloe—but she was terrifyingly competent and willing to point Chloe in the right direction with curriculum and government regulations. In Chloe's opinion that made her worth her weight in gold.

When number time and Sesame Street ended, it was time for group play. Maria and Mrs. Thompson organized the students into four groups and began the rotation between dress up, music, and manipulatives, while Chloe went to the kitchen to assemble the morning snacks.

Chapter 2

At 3:30, Tasha, the after-school helper, arrived. Maria and Chloe always looked forward to their first glimpse of Tasha's costume—costume being the only word to adequately describe her wardrobe.

Chloe wondered if she would have hired Tasha had she shown up for the interview in, say, her Goth outfit, but that would never have happened. Tasha was anything but foolish. That day had obviously been Mother's-Little-Helper day. She had arrived wearing an ankle-length denim jumper, embroidered with butterflies. The white blouse underneath had matching butterflies embroidered on the collar, and over the top she wore a pale yellow cardigan. Her hair had been caught back on the sides with sparkling butterfly barrettes, and on her feet were pink ballet slippers. Having been her employer for almost three months, Chloe knew no matter which outfit she chose, Tasha was always competent and fun with the children. They adored her.

A plus was that she also attended the prestigious Fowler Academy where Zach attended. Knowing someone had helped Zach's first days as a new kid at the end of the school year last spring, for which Chloe would forever be grateful. Since Tasha was a lot more forthcoming than Zach, Chloe counted on her for information about anything going on at school.

Today Tasha was Goth Girl. She wore a duster that was a clone of the one Zach had worn this morning. Under it, she wore black tights and a mid-thigh-length black sweater. Black Doc Martins were laced almost to her knee. Black eye makeup wreathed her eyes, and her hair was as black as the devil's soul. Often when she appeared straight from school, she also sported assorted piercings which Chloe insisted she remove before being around the children. The prospect of small fingers grabbing metal attachments made her shudder.

"Hi, Miss Chloe," Tasha's cheery voice didn't match her clothing, for which Chloe was glad. "Zach's coming. He and some guys were trying to master some kick flips, so he fell behind." She was almost three years older than Zach but as friendly as a puppy, and Zach thought she was the ultimate in cool.

While Tasha began doling out afternoon snacks, Chloe took the opportunity to step out the backdoor and check the progress. She gasped as she teetered at the doorsill, grabbing the sides of the door to gain her balance. While she had been busy teaching, answering phones, and tending to little people, Deke had also been busy—all of the walls, roof, and steps of the porch had disappeared. Deke turned his head at the sound and advised, "Watch where you step. I've tried very hard to not leave any nails lying around, but you don't want to jam one into your foot and end up with a tetanus shot or tetanus."

She carefully made her way off the porch. The floor was the only remnant of the broken-down extension that had clung to the back of the house like a barnacle on a rock. "You've been a lot busier than I expected." She eyed the industrial-sized dumpster that had been delivered that morning, piled high with broken boards, lathe and plaster, and shingles—all pieces of the walls and roof.

"Well," he drawled, taking off his ball cap, wiping his forehead with his forearm, and slapping the cap back on his head, "I have this nag of a boss. She's keeping me hopping."

She bit her lip to keep from grinning and moved around piles of rubble to stand beside him. Together they turned to silently view the house. After a moment of contemplation, he said, "I have to ask what made you decide to turn a historical gem like this into a day care? I would have thought that anything else would have been a better fit. You strike me as more of an interior decorator than babysitter."

She was swamped by her own memories and took a moment before replying, "Interior decorating businesses take too long to become income-producing, but a day care can do it in mere months if you are located in a good area.

"We bought this house because we planned to open a bed-and-breakfast business after Phillip retired. When Phillip's brother called about it, we couldn't resist the price, even though we wouldn't need it for at least two decades. We bought it and immediately found long-term renters, and basically put it out of our minds."

"What happened?" Unfortunately, he had a hollow feeling that it was divorce that had brought her and her son to Seattle. In his, admittedly, novice opinion, too many people didn't see marriage as a sacred vow between themselves and God. As soon as that thought appeared in his mind, he felt guilty – where did he get off judging someone without knowing the facts?

"Cancer happened," she said softly. "Phillip kept having back pain, and he lost his appetite. I convinced him to have his yearly physical early, and they found pancreatic cancer. Pancreatic cancer is especially aggressive, and most people die within six months." She swallowed past a lump and added, "Phillip was right on schedule."

He couldn't think of any words that wouldn't

sound banal, so didn't say anything. And his guilt this time came from his relief that she was a widow. No husband! No doubt about it, he was really a jerk.

She shifted, "Anyway, Phillip had to go on medical disability, and we weren't aware that when that happened, his company life insurance policy was canceled. Only after he died did I learn that Zach and I were broke, and I needed a way to support us, fast.

"The San Diego house no longer felt like home to either Zach or me, and both Phillip's family and mine live in Washington." She didn't add that Phillip's brother, Franklin, his only living relative whom she had counted on being in Seattle as a mentor to Zach, had been transferred by his company within weeks of their arrival. It was just one of those things that nobody could have foreseen, but if she'd known then what she knew now, she'd have moved them to Yakima to be near her family.

"We owned our house in San Diego free and clear, but this one still had a big mortgage. After looking at all the options, I decided it would be hard to unload this house, so I would keep it. I sold our California house for a whopping profit, and we moved here. This is both our home and a base for a business."

She changed the subject by waving her hand toward the back of the house, "What's the next step?"

"The foundation for the remainder of the sun room," he replied. The new addition would incorporate the space of the old porch, plus extend along the full length of the house. "I've ordered the joists and beams, and they'll be here by the end of this week, along with the lumber. By then, I will have set the footers for the foundation for the remainder of the sun room, and I can start framing it in.

She smiled, and he almost fell over at the sheer

impact of it turned on him, “The kids loved watching you tear stuff apart today, especially Daniel. His forte is demolition. I think he was born into the wrong family for the innate talents he seems to possess.”

He opened his mouth to ask about Daniel, but just then the teen he’d seen this morning came around the corner of the house and stopped in shock, “Whoa! What happened, Mom?” He still looked like a stinker to Deke, who kept quiet and shamelessly eavesdropped.

“Zach, I told you the remodeling was beginning today. That’s why I insisted you help me unload the porch last night. I’d like you to meet Mr. Hudson, the contractor for the job. He’s the one you almost knocked over today as you barreled out the door.”

Zach had the grace to flush. He lowered his head, nodded to Deke, and muttered, “Pleased to meet you.”

Deke crossed the few feet that separated them, hand outstretched, “Hello, Zach, call me Deke.”

Zach took his hand briefly, and then turned back to his mom, “What time’s dinner, Mom?”

“If you’re willing to eat early, I can feed you at five, just before I leave. If you plan on skating awhile, I’ll leave yours in the oven. I want you to promise that you will be home by seven. I am only staying at the center until eight o’clock so when I get home I expect you to be here and to have eaten.

It was hard to tell through the scowl, but Deke thought he saw a flicker of disappointment in Zach’s eyes before he said, “I’m going to grab a snack and meet the guys at the park.” He disappeared into the kitchen.

She sighed. She really, really missed the twelve-year-old Zach. That Zach, even grieving over his dad’s death, had been talkative, funny, and loving. This thirteen-year-old model was very hard to deal with. She had tried her hardest to accommodate his grief, even going against her better judgment and allowing him to fit in with the kids at the skate park with his (to her opinion) horrible wardrobe and hair style. Yet still he remained emotionally inaccessible.

What irritated her even more was her hesitation to confront his moods. She was afraid one wrong move on her part would spark the rebellion she could see simmering just below the surface.

Zach reappeared almost immediately, an apple in one hand, a fistful of cookies in the other, and his skateboard tucked under his arm, "I'll try and make five o'clock; depends on who's at the park," he said unconcernedly. He plopped the skateboard onto the driveway, mounted it, and rolled out of sight.

She turned away from his figure, filled with frustration and despair and caught Deke's somber gaze. The sympathy in his gaze, unlike this morning, suddenly made her mad, "We're doing fine, Mr. Hudson," she snapped. "He is just at a difficult age."

She was disconcerted by his mild response, "It's Deke, and I wasn't finding fault with you. Raising a teen is hard for everyone."

At that moment Tasha appeared in the doorway and diverted their attention, "Miss Chloe, there's water flowing down the hallway."

Chloe shot into the house. Sure enough, a lake was spreading rapidly from under the boys' bathroom door. She pushed open the door to view the toilet overflowing.

Deke brushed past her and squatted by the toilet. He reached behind, twisted a knob, and immediately the water quit pouring over the top of the bowl. "Boy, he's good." Deke's voice held admiration, "What do you suppose he flushed down it?"

"Daniel?" she asked. As if there could be any doubt about the perpetrator.

"Ask him so I'll know what I'm fishing for."

She sighed, "Daniel?" She cocked her head toward the doorway and waited. A moment passed then a small figure approached warily, "Que pasa?" His expression was sweetly inquiring.

Deke hid a grin, but Chloe was made of sterner stuff, "Daniel, did you put something in the toilet today?"

"Uh-huh, these," and he thrust a handful of Legos toward her.

She groaned, and Deke laughed. He got to work while she rounded up the mop and bucket. Tasha expertly collected the children together in the other room, promising them a story. Chloe blessed her good fortune in finding such a talented teen for a helper.

Deke was as an efficient plumber for a carpenter, and within twenty minutes he had the bathroom operational. As she rinsed out the mop in the laundry room, she apologized, "I'm so sorry. You were hired to remodel not to be the resident plumber."

"Just glad I was here," was his comfortable response.

Chapter 3

Chloe left work at four-thirty, leaving Tasha to lock up after the last child was checked out. She was pleased that a prospective couple had stopped by to view the business as a possible day care for their four-year-old twins. Both parents were doctors working on Pill Hill—Seattle's name for the nearby complex of medical facilities. If she signed a contract for their care she would be at capacity, having done the unthinkable in just over four months—running in the black.

Climbing the stairs to their apartment, she ignored the nagging sadness that hit her. There were so many times when she felt isolated and alone. She missed Phillip, but at least it wasn't the gaping wound it had been for so many months.

Entering the front door, the quiet, empty apartment was oppressive. She marched directly to the kitchen, pulled open the freezer, and grabbed the carton of her favorite ice cream off the top shelf. En route to the table, she lifted a spoon from the drawer and snagged the phone off the wall. Plopping into a chair, she tore off the lid, stuck in her spoon, and punched speed dial for Maddie.

Maddie answered on the first ring, "Hi, sweetie, how are you doing?" Thank goodness for caller I.D. The warmth in her little sister's voice already made her feel better. Two years younger, they'd been best friends since the day Mom and Dad brought her home. Chloe had thought they'd brought her a real live doll to play with.

"I'm eating Haagen Dazs Banana Split straight from the carton," Chloe informed her as she stuck another spoonful into her mouth. The cream and sugar was already giving her a lift.

Laughter floated over the line, "Day that bad?" Her voice took on an innocence that didn't fool Chloe, "It shouldn't have been too bad of a day—wasn't today the day the remodeler started?"

Chloe groaned. In a moment of weakness, she had confided to Maddie her silly attraction. She ignored the subtle dig, "No, I'm just sad and frustrated."

"I'm sorry sweetie. What's Zach up to now?"

"He's fine," she swallowed a lump and refused to allow the sound of tears to show in her voice. "Skateboarding every spare minute he has. But right now he's mad at me because I have to go out tonight. I don't know why he cares, I can't say he misses us spending time together because, when we are, we're either fighting or in separate parts of the house."

Another quarter cup of creamy goodness made its way down her throat.

"Now, Chloe, Zach's supposed to be mad at you. He's a teenager. It's the kiss of death to like your parents at thirteen."

Maddie had three children, and her oldest son, Ryan, was four months older than Zach. The boys were as different as night and day yet as close as tape stuck to a wall. In an attempt to help Zach acclimate to the move, Chloe had allowed him to spend most of the summer in Yakima. Ryan had taken him to all the 4-H activities that were a big part of his life in a rural community, and Zach had introduced him to skateboarding. Since school started they hadn't been able to get together, but she knew for a fact that he and Ryan emailed each other continually.

"He just won't talk to me," she hated sounding so needy, "and I still don't know any of his friends."

"That's the hardest for you isn't it?" Maddie's voice was kind. She knew how much Chloe had invested into being a good mother.

"Yes, it is. I need to be involved in his life and know who his friends are, at this age more than any other."

"Chloe, I don't think him not bringing friends over is because he suddenly doesn't like you; I think it's the contrast to what his family is now—just the two of you—from what it was when Phillip was still alive. That is still too fresh a pain in him."

"Well, what should I do? If I could bring Phillip back, I assure I would do that," she knew her tone was acerbic.

Maddie's voice was affectionate, "Ice cream must be bringing your sugar level up; you're back to your old cranky self." There was a pause, then she ventured, "One thing you could try is to quit overindulging him."

"I don't overindulge him," Chloe muttered, hoping the lightning that was sure to strike would not be a direct hit.

"Uh-huh," Maddie's tone was firm, "you do Chloe, and it's so unlike you. I have to say the purple Mohawk we saw on Labor Day is a definite change in your parenting style."

"It's just that he's lost so much," she hated the sound of tears in her voice, "and he's trying to fit in with his friends at the skate park. Having a Mohawk does not mean my son's a hood."

"No, it certainly doesn't, but the Mohawk highlights the underlying problem. You're giving into his demands because you feel guilty Phillip is gone. You can't give him back his dad, and indulgences are not a healthy substitute."

"I know," she sighed. Her family had hinted several times how concerned they were over her sudden lenience with Zach. In truth, it was such a contradiction of her personality, even she was surprised.

They spoke for a few more minutes, not returning to the subject of Zach. Chloe related the Daniel crisis, looking for a laugh, and Maddie didn't disappoint.

"Well, you have Daniel, and I have Mom."

Chloe sighed. People who came into contact with Faith McKinnon Dyer used terms like effervescent, bubbly, darling, and delightful. And while Chloe adored her mother, she knew she needed a good grasp on her nerves and a calm stomach to deal with her. Today had been too stressful. Faith was not for the weak-hearted.

"Okay, what's up with Mom?"

"Well," Maddie's voice grew cozy, "it started with Mrs. Pritchet's boxer." Mrs. Pritchet had lived on the opposite end of the block from their parents as far back as Chloe could remember. She'd been a widow that long, too, and, having no children, she'd had a succession of dogs that she treated better than most people treated their kids.

"Okay," Chloe was keeping up, "Mrs. Pritchet's spoiled, mean boxer, who is called, why no one will ever know, Tummie."

"Because he likes to have his tummy scratched," Maddie replied absently, "but that's not the point. Tummie got into Dad's flowerbed again, began to dig, and Dad went out with the BB-gun and shot his rear. Tummie went yelping home, and almost immediately, Mrs. Pritchet came roaring down the street. So she and Dad got into a yelling match about her dog, and she threatened to sue Dad, and Dad threatened to use live ammo next time." She got sidetracked; in Maddie's case the apple didn't fall from the tree, "What's considered live ammo for a BB gun?"

Sometimes Maddie had to be helped over the line, so Chloe hardly paused at the non sequitur, "I don't know. Go on, what happened next? I know the next installment features Mom; just tell me."

"Well, Mom separated them, got Dad settled down, and then decided that what made Tummie so mean was that he didn't have any companions. So she talked Mrs. Pritchet into going to the pound with her, and she adopted a terrier mix. Now Tummie won't leave the yard because he's afraid the terrier will steal all his toys, and everyone is happy."

"Well, everyone except for Tummie, that is," Chloe felt forced to point out.

"Yes, but Mom convinced Mrs. Pritchet his anti-social behavior was because he'd never been canine socialized, and that was why he roamed—seeking it."

"And she bought that?"

"Of course! It came from Faith McKinnon Dyer; anything she says sounds reasonable until you analyze it, and by then, she's gone and you're stuck."

"Maddie?"

"Umm?"

"How will we ever be able to tell if Mom gets Alzheimer's?" They were both silent, contemplating this puzzle then burst into giggles simultaneously.

"Thanks, sis, I needed that laugh," Chloe wiped her eyes.

"I know. You're lucky to have me for a sister."

"I know, and the fact that you remind me of it over and over is a big help."

"Always glad to help out. Now don't finish off the carton. Go eat some real food"

As she hung up the phone, she was smiling. She had survived a day with Deke without revealing her attraction to him or her sister. Of the two, Maddie was the harder one to fool. Since she and Zach had moved to Seattle, Maddie had been encouraging her to get involved in something that would allow her to meet people her own age. By *people*, Chloe knew she meant men. She was sure Maddie would approve of Deke.

She felt a soft brush around her feet and glanced down to see Maleficent doing her dead cat imitation. Maleficent was a pure-bred Abyssinian that Mom had gotten at the shelter the same day she had showed up to help them unpack. Only Mom would have thought a gift cat was exactly what they needed the first day in their Seattle home. Because Zach had shown the first sign of animation in days, she had caved and let Maleficent stay.

Maleficent loved attention, and her favorite ploy was to simply fall onto her side beside whomever was nearest, in hopes they would take pity and pet her. Automatically, Chloe began to move her foot back and forth across the cat's fur, and Maleficent rotated her body to get the maximum satisfaction from the massage.

"You are a worthless piece of fur," she crooned, and Maleficent opened her topaz eyes a slit to glare at the interruption. "Okay, your highness, I can't stand here all day," she moved her foot whereupon Maleficent meowed and stalked away.

She had stew and sub sandwiches ready at five, but Zach didn't appear. She ate hers, putting his meal aside.

At six, she exited the house for her meeting. Deke was busy loading tools into his pickup and didn't appear to notice her leaving.

The prenatal class at the Life Center was busy, and she enrolled eleven young women for the six-week course. After the first session began, she went into the office and finished some book work that she had left undone the previous week. Like all non-profit organizations, volunteers were its life blood. She had come highly recommended from a sister Life Center in California and easily accepted similar responsibilities she had been accustomed to in San Diego. At seven-forty-five she left to go back home.

###

The apartment was dark when she entered it at eight, and her heart pounded, "Zach?" she called. Surely he was home now. But walking through all the rooms testified to his absence. She searched the table for a note he may have left. Just as she was contemplating getting into her car to find him, Zach came through the door.

Bolstered by her anger and the earlier conversation with Maddie, Chloe was ready to take him on. She eyed him coolly, arms crossed. This was the first time he hadn't come home when she'd instructed. Her family was right; she'd better take back her son before she lost him entirely. He was becoming a stranger. They had both been altered by Phillip's death: She, once a hard-nosed no-nonsense mother, had acquired a noodle spine, waffling over every decision and caving to Zach's demands. Zach had changed from an easy-going youngster into a surly oaf.

He glanced at her but didn't give any explanation for where he'd been or why he had missed supper. She uncrossed her arms, took a deep breath to control the urge to clamp her hands around his neck and squeeze, and said evenly, "You need to be home for dinner every night unless we make other arrangements. You are not old enough to decide for yourself where you're going to be and what you're going to do. Do you understand?"

His back was to hers as he leaned into the refrigerator. She thought she heard a grunt and took a deep breath. *Don't back off now. Just because you've folded like a limp paper bag in the past, doesn't mean you can't regain ground.* "Zach," her voice now dripped with icicles, "I said, 'Do you understand?'"

He straightened and faced her, "Yes, ma'am, I heard you."

She eyed his demeanor, looking for signs of rebellion, but only saw his sadness. Once again, her heart clenched, and she was ready to forgive him anything, "Zach, we have to work together. I don't know the kids you hang out with, I don't even know what you do when you're gone. Are you really skating, or are you doing something else?"

His eyes widened, "I'm skating, Mom. And I don't go anywhere else than the skate park. I just forgot the time. We were trying to work on our ollies, and before I knew it, it was already eight o'clock." He ducked his head, "'Sides I hate coming home when you aren't here."

Her heart broke at this admission. She had never known he didn't like her not being around. Now that she thought about it, when she had volunteered before, he and his dad had done things together. She obviously needed to rethink her priorities.

He spoke up, "If you'd get me my own cell phone, you could find out where I was at any time." He had made that argument quite a few times already. Now she began to understand that giving him a cell phone could work in her favor.

She nodded, "I guess you're right. Okay, we'll go tomorrow after school and get you a cell phone. But," she leveled a finger at him, "I expect that phone to be on all the time you're out of school and that you will promise to answer it every time I call you. Otherwise, no phone. And since you deliberately disobeyed me tonight, you will not go anywhere after school for a week."

Evidently the phone was more than compensation for any pain because Zach's grin was filled with delight, "Okay, whatever. Can I get a phone with unlimited texting?"

"Don't push it, buster."

At that moment, Maleficent wandered into the kitchen and wound herself around Zach's legs. He scooped her up and hugged her to his chest, rubbing her ears and sharing the great news of his phone. Chloe walked out, squashing the urge to offer to fix Zach some late supper. He was old enough to find something on his own.

###

She went to bed at ten p.m., pausing to knock on Zach's door and call out goodnight. He'd called back over the sounds of his war game.

She lay in bed for a few minutes contemplating Zach's candid remark. He had inadvertently revealed something, and she would be a fool to overlook it. She volunteered for a variety of reasons—social consciousness, a cause she believed in, and fulfillment—

but none of them were important enough to take the place of caring for her son. She definitely needed to cut back drastically on volunteering so that she could be home for Zach.

For some reason, her last thought before falling asleep was Deke. She wondered if he was married and if he had any children. She reminded herself that she had no business thinking about another man. She was a mother of a teenager and the sole provider for them both; that was all the complications she needed in her life.

Chapter 4

It was just before seven o'clock that same evening when Deke pulled into his driveway. He had had to run by the lumber company on his way home, so it was later than usual. He unloaded the tools and re-locked the pickup. Entering the back door of his house, he was almost knocked down by Woofer, his ecstatic mixed-breed. "Hi, guy," he rubbed his ears. "You miss me?" He knew, despite the dog's poor-me demeanor, that he had been fine. He had built Woofer a doggie door so he could come and go as he wished.

Woofer was a party animal and usually accompanied him to his jobs, so he hadn't taken kindly to being left home today. Deke knew that he had to get a feel for this new job first. He hoped to convince Chloe that Woofer would be a positive addition to The Perfect Child job. The kids would love watching Woof out the window of the play room, just as they had spent most of the day watching him. Woofer was leash trained and a real gentleman.

He had found the (mostly) Airedale hiding in the bushes three blocks from his home approximately four years ago. He had been cold and hungry and trying, unsuccessfully, to keep out of the rain. If he had ever had a master, it had been some time ago; his ribs stood in stark relief against his matted coat. The patient acceptance of his bleak life in his brown eyes had tugged at Deke, and he loaded the dog in his truck and took him home. After toweling him dry, Deke fed him the leftover steak originally planned for his own supper—it disappeared in two gulps—then placed a blanket in the corner on which the dog had promptly curled up and gone to sleep. Woofer moved in and never left.

Deke dropped his lunch pail and clipboard on the kitchen table, checked to make sure Woofer's food and water bowls were still full, and re-exited the back door. Woofer followed closely as he walked across his back patio, crossing to the property on the south side. He sighed soundlessly at the satisfaction owning his own property gave him. Growing up in foster homes, he would never have thought he'd be a homeowner. And he certainly wouldn't have achieved it without David and Bea's intervention in his life. He never took for granted how God had blessed him.

Fremont was a neighborhood of upper middle class homes, most of them built before 1940. He found this run-down property when first scouting for a location for his business, and to his amazement he'd been the lowest bidder when the estate went into foreclosure at the owner's death. It had been Mr. Evans' brother Franklin who had helped him close the deal and, he imagined, recommended him to Chloe for her remodeling. So happy to be a property owner, Deke hadn't even minded living in the shop during the year it had taken him to gut the interior and remodel.

Crossing his neighbor's driveway, he mounted the steps, knocked briefly on the back door, opened it, and stepped into the kitchen. Woofer, knowing he wasn't allowed inside, curled up on the top step to wait.

It made a profound statement about how close he had become to Mrs. Watanabe that she allowed him to walk into her home without waiting for a formal invitation. The reserved Japanese widow had aloofness down to a fine art until she considered someone a close friend. Although she had lived in America for over five decades and run a prosperous Chinese restaurant for most of that time, she still wore her dignified manner tightly wrapped around her like a cloak. It had taken her a while to thaw to him, but once she had, he was family.

Deke enjoyed his diminutive neighbor and patiently bore her scolding. Her fractured English didn't inhibit her ability to list the multitude of ways he was a failure—ranging from not taking care of himself, to not searching for a wife. Her pithy assessment of his pitiful life reminded him of how an aunt or grandmother would have worried about him, had he been fortunate enough to have either one. He liked it.

He made sure she kept her doctors' appointments—although, at seventy-two her health was probably better than his—delivered her to her monthly meetings with friends in the Japanese community, and undertook the ongoing repairs necessary to maintain her old home.

In return, she offered him a version of family, a surrogate aunt with whom he enjoyed cutthroat games of Mah Jong and the History channel—except anything to do with World War II, of course. The Watanabes hadn't immigrated to the United States until the early 1950s, and the subject of world history seemed better left alone. As a bonus, she kept him supplied with egg rolls and invited him for sushi at least twice a month. It was a good trade off.

"Egg rolls?" he'd queried the first time she served them, raising an eyebrow, "*Chinese* eggrolls?"

Her stiff little face hadn't changed, but her eyes had twinkled, "Japanese steakhouses were unknown when Dai and I came to the United States. The only oriental food the round-eyes wanted was Chinese, so all Asians had Chinese restaurants, whether we were Japanese or Thai." She nodded at the pile of paper-thin, crispy rolls in the middle of the table, "So, yes, *Chinese* eggrolls, and they are the best in Seattle."

She was one of the reasons, albeit not the most important reason, he worked four days a week. Every Monday morning at six o'clock sharp, rain or shine—but usually rain in Seattle—he and Mrs. Watanabe headed to Pike's Place Market. "I don't want the leftovers," she insisted when questioned why so early. For someone who barely rose above his belt buckle, she could boss with the best. With him holding the bags, he trailed behind the tiny woman attired in black pants and a tunic, her head covered by a white kerchief, as they visited the fish mongers just as they were unloading their first catch of the week. From there they stopped by the vegetable farmers, adding herbs and piles of red, gold, and bright green veggies to the bags. She was implacable in her standards and harangued more than one merchant into giving up their very best to her. He had learned about the multitude of mushrooms and their specialties. He had eaten more varieties of seafood than he had ever known existed and thoroughly enjoyed his education.

Now he heard her delicate little shuffle across the living room floor as she came to greet him. "Those kids were back again today," she announced as she entered the kitchen.

He stifled a groan as his concern went up a notch. Unsupervised groups of teens could morph into trouble in a heartbeat. And apparently a group of them had found the empty ground at the back of his property interesting. He had scouted the area each time she had seen them but so far hadn't caught them. It unsettled him that she was an elderly woman alone with what amounted to a teenage gang rambling outside her property.

"It's beginning to be every day isn't it?" He wiped his hand across his face, "Maybe I'd better start coming home early for a few days and see if I can catch them on the property." He could imagine how well that would go over with Mrs. Evans.

She folded her arms, "And upset Ms. Uptight, even more?" He had told her about Chloe, embellishing on her uptight tendencies, and Mrs. Watanabe had begun calling her by that label.

He grinned, "Yes, she'll be thrilled. Although, I'm beginning to think her bark is bigger than her bite; this is more important. What age do you think they are?" Even ten-year-olds in a pack could wreak havoc, but the potential was greater if they were middle school kids. Middle school age was dangerous with the onset of puberty but no outlet, such as jobs or cars, to distract them.

"Probably about Asuka's age." Her granddaughter was twelve, so they must be middle schoolers. "What do you mean her bark is bigger than her bite?"

"Well, she certainly has a problem with me, but she's sweet as pie to her charges."

Mrs. Watanabe's face got crafty, "Maybe she's attracted to you and uncomfortable with it."

He snorted, "Well if that's the way attraction works on her, it's mighty confusing. Besides, I wouldn't be interested in someone with a rebellious teen. We'd clash big time over parenting styles. Her kid is a nightmare."

He shook his head at his neighbor in mild reproof, "Stop trying to marry me off. It might backfire on you, you know. I could fall in love and marry someone who lives in California, and then who would take care of you?"

"The same person who's taken care of me for 72 years – me!"

Since there wasn't a resolution for this age-old argument, he was glad to drop it and accept her invitation to supper. Unfortunately, he knew from experience that she had only shelved it; it would be brought up again.

It was nine o'clock before he left, after a supper of miso soup and turbot and a host of last-minute reminders from Mrs. Watanabe about getting to the ferry the next morning. The ferry to Victoria, British Columbia, was a favorite excursion for the residents of Seattle. Every fall, Mrs. Watanabe and several of her friends took the ferry to enjoy a few days in the beautiful city. They stayed at the Empress Hotel, enjoyed High Tea in the lobby, took a bus ride out to Butchart Gardens, and generally had themselves a high old time. He assured her he'd be at her front door bright and early and left for home, collecting Woofer off the step.

Just to see if he could find any evidence of what kept drawing the kids to his property, he grabbed a flashlight from his truck cab and walked the perimeter of both his and Mrs. Watanabe's lots. Not for the first time, he wished he had enough money to fence his whole property, but with almost an acre of land, the cost was beyond his means. Woofer plodded silently beside him.

Any empty ground in the Northwest was soon covered by wild blackberry bushes, growing in an impenetrable hedge, sometimes as tall as twenty feet. Most of his lot was cleared to make room for his house and outbuildings, plus the piles of materials he used for his work, but at the back of the property, the land he wasn't using was filled with the bushes. They weren't a total nuisance, as he enjoyed the fruit from them and the privacy they offered. However, he was aware that the thicket could be used as a hiding place for more than raccoons and squirrels.

As he skirted the blackberry bushes on the perimeter, he saw where a trail had been pushed out. Curious to see if it was simply a shortcut through his property or something else, he pushed his way in, ignoring the brambles as they grabbed his shirt and pants. A few more feet and he reached a clearing where the branches had been flattened to make a small fort. This was new, and he didn't like it. His light illuminated the space, estimating it to be approximately ten-by-ten feet. If they were too old to be elementary-age children, he didn't want to imagine what they could be using the space for. The only reason for teens to be hiding would be for criminal or immoral purposes, and he didn't need it happening on his property where he could be liable.

A blue, plastic ground tarp, probably one of his, was rigged among the branches to create some protection from the ever-present northwest rain. He frowned and looked around, but they hadn't left any evidence that would identify who was here. He couldn't estimate how long they had been using his property, but he knew it was ending today. He headed to his shop to build No Trespassing signs to hang along the edge of his property. It was past ten before he had them constructed and posted. As he put his tools away, he hoped the signs would be a sufficient warning, and he wouldn't see any more indication of trespassers.

Before turning in, he spent his final hour in his office, printing out billing invoices and arranging for the shipping of a beautiful set of end tables to Texas. It was with satisfaction that he surveyed his accounts. Not too far ahead was the day he could support himself totally on his furniture business.

"And you too, Woofer," he crooned to his dog lying like a burlap rug at his feet. "Gotta keep you in biscuits, huh?" From the devotion in Woofer's eyes, he believed anything Deke attempted was possible.

His last thought before sleep captured him was of the fire in Chloe's hair as she stood outside in the afternoon sunlight.

Chapter 5

Deke pulled up to Mrs. Watanabe's at five a.m. the next morning, before the sun had decided to peek out from under its covers. She was watching for him and was on the porch before he had even gotten out of the Jeep. As she traversed the steps, holding her purse that was as big as Texas, he hauled the wooden steps out of the back of his Cherokee and placed them in front of the passenger side door, assisting her as she climbed into the wagon. He hefted her suitcase into the back, and they were off on their appointed rounds.

Forty minutes later, after three other stops each time hauling out the steps and helping tiny, elderly Asians climb into the vehicle, he hit the freeway and headed for the ferry terminal. There, he parked in front, unloaded his passengers, helped the red cap stack the luggage on a cart, tipped him generously so he'd keep an eye on them until they were seated in the ferry lounge, and submitted to hugs and kisses from four diminutive septuagenarians.

He straightened from the last hug and leveled a stern finger at them, "I will be here to pick you up Sunday night, and I don't want to hear that any of you were arrested for wild behavior." He smiled as they fluttered into the terminal, giggling and chattering away in Japanese, looking, in their uniform black and white, like small emperor penguins from the back.

Back in his truck, he realized it wasn't yet six, and while it might be too early to begin hammering and sawing, there were other, quieter chores he could begin;

he decided to go to work. He exited the freeway to swing past his house, where he garaged the Cherokee and loaded the truck. Looking at Woofer's sad face he consoled, "I promise to ask if you can come with me tomorrow, okay?" With his tools in the back, he pointed the pickup toward Queen Anne.

As he pulled into the back of the day care, he realized he'd never gotten a key to the house and would have to ring the doorbell. He momentarily caved, after all it was early, but he couldn't resist. He rounded the house, climbed the front steps two at a time, and thumbed the doorbell until a window above his head was shoved open. Hard.

"Hello?" The groggy greeting assured him that he had roused her from sleep.

He stepped back from under the porch overhang and angled his head up to view her scowl. He smiled. Big. "Good morning. I forgot to get a key yesterday so I will need you to let me in and hopefully give me a spare key so I don't have to wake you again." He really had meant to sound regretful, but the spark from those greens was too much temptation to resist.

She slammed her window shut. He cooled his heels for a couple of minutes until she stood in the doorway, "Coffee on?" he inquired as he brushed past her.

Her glare should have brought him to his knees, "It's barely dawn, I am not up, and no, there isn't any coffee.

He led the way into the day care kitchen, "Huh, don't have one of those automatic pots? I pegged you as a lady who needed caffeine first thing."

She sighed, "My automatic pot goes off upstairs,

and Maria has early shift, not me." She jerked her head toward the counter, "If you want coffee, the makings are over there. Help yourself." So stating, she turned to leave, pausing in the doorway, "And I will get you a key today." He grinned as she about-faced and stomped out. Son-of-a-gun it was fun to pull her chain.

Forty minutes later, Maria and Deke, both of them on their second cup of java—him after unloading his truck and she taking a break from checking in toddlers—looked up as Chloe and Zach barged into the room arguing. They observed the exchange between mother and son as if they had front-row seats at the circus.

Chloe wrenched open a cupboard door, extracted a bowl, and slammed it shut. It immediately bounced open again from the impact, "You need to eat breakfast, and I'm tired of bugging you about it young man." She reached into a second cupboard and slammed down a box of cereal. She turned to the fridge for fruit and a carton of milk, "From now on, you will get up early enough to eat breakfast, or I will take your skateboard away."

Zach was shocked. His jaw dropped, and his face reddened, "You and whose army?" he yelled.

In a heartbeat Deke straightened from a lounge against the counter to his full six feet two inches and loomed over Chloe to speak to Zach, "You apologize to your mom, or it will be me who takes your skateboard away."

She ignored how good it felt to have someone behind her, standing up for her, and forged ahead, intent on getting her son's attention, "I don't need an army Zacheus Phillip Evans. I will take your skateboard beginning tomorrow if I don't get your promise to eat breakfast and to be home for dinner every night. Do you understand me?"

Zach was sullen, "Okay, okay, man. Chill will you? I'll be home by six-thirty tonight, and I'll eat breakfast every morning. Satisfied?"

"Yes," she spoke at the same moment that Deke stated, "No." He continued, "Apologize for speaking to your mom in that tone of voice."

Zach eyed the tall man and wisely decided not to push the issue, "Sorry, Mom."

"You're forgiven."

The silence was a thick blanket while Zach gulped down his cereal in record time. He grabbed up his backpack and skateboard and hit the back door. The slam of the door echoed in the silence but didn't block the sound of a crash as he evidently miscalculated the height off the back porch without the back steps. A moment later, the slap of his skateboard wheels, hitting the driveway, drifted back as he rolled out of earshot.

Chloe turned to face Deke, fire still in her eyes, "I do not need help raising my son. He's going through a difficult time right now, but we are fine." She thrust back the thought of how good it had been to have someone stand up for her, someone to help hold the line with a teen.

He shrugged. "Didn't look fine from where I was standing, and you've got the wrong man if you expect me to stand aside while your son abuses you."

Chloe gasped in shock, "Zach wasn't abusing me."

"Yes, he is."

From his uncompromising tone and at the serious head nod from Maria in agreement, Chloe slumped against the counter. Her chin wobbled, and she blinked furiously to stem the advancing tears.

Deke appeared not to notice, "But you are right; it is none of my business. Now, if you ladies will excuse me, I have work to do."

As he turned away, Daniel burst through the doorway, shouting, "Miss Chloe! Miss Maria!" He was shadowed by his father, who smiled in relief when he saw them.

Daniel, spotting Deke, was abruptly silenced.

"Good morning, Daniel," Chloe's voice was the voice of angels. Deke looked at her in disbelief. If she ever spoke to him in that voice, he'd...well, he didn't know what he'd do, but glancing at the object of her attention, he decided that he'd probably look as besotted as the preschooler.

Daniel smiled at her greeting, but his gaze was riveted on Deke, who suppressed a grin. He could have told Miss Chloe there wasn't a teacher, no matter how pretty, that was adequate enticement to draw a preschooler away from a tool belt.

Daniel's gaze zeroed in on the shiny pointy metal objects so tantalizingly within reach. His arm seemed to rise of its own volition as he stretched to touch the tool belt strapped around Deke's middle. "Is that a tape measure?" Awe filled his gruff little voice, "What are you going to measure? May I hold the end of the tape for you?" The visions of hammers and saws dancing in his head were almost visible to the eye.

Chloe sighed, "Good morning, Daniel." She firmly grasped his shoulders and turned him toward Maria, "Go with Miss Maria and help check yourself in. You may not stay; we have grown-up work to do." Deke expected an argument, but Daniel was evidently used to disappointment over his optimistic plans, because after a last lingering look at the shiny hardware, he trotted off holding Maria's hand, his dad trailing after him.

She watched to make sure Daniel carried through on the order, and Deke took the opportunity to observe her again. He didn't understand his fascination with her; sure she was attractive, but it was something more than that. He estimated her to be two or three years older than him, which would make her thirty-three or thirty-four. He'd never considered that he could be attracted to an older woman and that amused him.

Unnerved by his gaze, Chloe gave Deke the eye, and he grinned, gave her a casual salute, and left the kitchen to cross the porch floor and spring agilely to the ground, not stumbling as Zach had done.

"What's his story?" Maria spoke over her shoulder.

Startled, Chloe turned to her, "Well, he's a carpenter and likes good coffee."

Maria, snorted, "You think I don't see how the two of you look at each other when you think the other one doesn't know it?"

Chloe laughed in spite of herself. "He's the remodeler, Maria, not a prospective date. I don't have his story." Noticing her speculative look, she added, "And while he may or may not be married, you are." Maria laughed. She had offered more than once to fix Chloe up with one of her many cousins. So far Chloe had managed to avoid meeting any of them, but she didn't expect Maria to back off. Happily-married women, of whom she used to be one, were notorious for wanting the entire world's population to pair off.

Maria sobered and looked her in the eye. "Chloe, it's okay. You're beginning to wake up, and that's good. You're young. You have much to give someone, and even though I never met your Phillip, I know he would want you to move on."

Chloe felt tears well up in her eyes, "Then why does it feel like betrayal?"

Maria gathered her close in a warm embrace, "Because it's a new beginning, sweetie. Anything new feels unsettling at first. Give yourself a chance to see where this will go." She left the kitchen, leaving Chloe standing in silence.

The daily activities at the Perfect Child proceeded uneventfully. Maria taught music and story time, and Mrs. Thompson did a baking activity with the children. They both oversaw lunch, and afterwards Mrs. Thompson set up the afternoon activities, while Maria read to them during nap time and Chloe escaped to her office to do paperwork. After only four months, she could proceed through her day by rote and refused to look at the years of the same activities stretching endlessly before her.

All was serene until she sensed someone's presence and looked up to see Deke in her doorway, Daniel tucked under his arm. She sprang up, horrified, "Daniel! How did you get outside?"

"I used the handle of the broom to hold down the bell, so I could open the door," his expression said *duh.* "The other kids were sleeping, Miss Chloe, I didn't want to wake them."

Deke set Daniel on his feet, Daniel chattering excitedly, "Miss Chloe, did you know Mr. Deke has powerful tools?" His blissful expression made her blood run cold.

She knelt before him and looked him in the eye, "Daniel. You are never to look at, touch, hold, or use any of Mr. Deke's tools. They are very, very dangerous. You would hurt yourself, and your daddy would cry, and Miss Chloe would cry, and Miss Maria would cry, and Mrs. Thompson would cry and Miss Tasha…"

"Okay," Daniel got the idea, "but Miss Chloe, would you ask my daddy to get me some tools? Mr. Deke's are really cool."

Holding Daniel's hand, Chloe escorted him back to his sleeping cot. Maria looked up at their entrance, a horrified expression on her face. She glanced over at his empty pad, with its rumpled blanket, "Oh, Chloe, when did that happen? I never saw him leave."

Chloe smiled, she tucked Daniel back in his cot, making sure that his stuffed elephant was close at hand, and shook her head at Maria, "I know, I know. Angels work overtime when assigned to Daniel. He only went outside to use Mr. Deke's powerful tools."

They gazed at each other as the full impact of what could have happened hit them. Something had to be done about Daniel. He was enchanting, maddening, and thoroughly lovable, but if any harm came to him on her watch, she'd never forgive herself.

She returned to her office to find Deke still waiting, his amusement evident, "What's Daniel's story?"

"He's a four-year-old genius."

"Maybe your four-year-old genius' parents need to find another day care for him."

"This four-year-old-genius moved my business into the profit column all by himself." She glanced at him, "His dad is Malcolm Pendergraff."

"Oh." Everyone in Seattle knew the name Malcolm Pendergraff, Microsoft's newest whiz kid. They'd hired him away from HP and the London office. According to the Seattle Times, he was a widower with one child, a genius, and quite obviously, that was Daniel.

She grinned, "You saw him; how could anyone turn that adorable child away? It's impossible to be mad at him; he so definitely doesn't mean to be naughty. And the fact that he's been kicked out the best preschools in King County meant I could name my price. His dad's bonus allowed me to hire extra help, because we needed more eyes on this little whiz kid."

Since arriving four months ago after—she found out later—being asked to leave from no less than four other day cares in the area, Daniel had dismantled the front door locks, escaping to the front gate before she caught up with him; removed all the knobs on the television, VCRs, and stereo in the music center; and dismantled the chandelier above the reading center—they hadn't discovered how he'd climbed ten feet off the floor, because he had done it during nap time. Craft time was a study in creativity—glue and crayons and paper did not hold Daniel's interest; however, scissors drew him as surely as the north drew a magnet, anything that could be broken down and reassembled fascinated him, and absolutely anything with a nut and bolt was not safe around his inspection.

At the end of the first frazzled week with Daniel, she had met Malcolm at the door with a look in her eye he had evidently recognized—probably the four previous times he'd been asked to find another place for Daniel.

"Miss Chloe," he smiled weakly, "please don't say that Daniel has to leave. He loves you and The Perfect Child day care. He's been much better behaved here, too; you must have an admirably alert staff."

She had eyed Malcolm. She saw a medium-height, thirty-year-old nerd—cardigan sweater, pocket protector, black-framed eyeglasses broken and mended with tape.

Pudgy Daniel was his clone, except for the pocket protector and that, at the moment, his wire-rimmed eyeglasses weren't broken.

"Daniel is a delight," she began and watched Malcolm swell up like a pouter pigeon, "and I know he doesn't mean to be destructive, but I have had to take child-proofing to a whole new level in the week since he's arrived."

Malcolm nodded enthusiastically, proud of her pro-active measures, "Surely, now that you know how inquisitive he is, you have shut all the loopholes. I imagine he won't be able to find anything else to take apart to discover how it works."

Chloe turned her attention from her reverie and back to Deke, " I'd hoped the new safety measures would be sufficient to contain Daniel. Any suggestions you can give me would be greatly appreciated."

He nodded. During the hours he had already spent on the property, Deke had observed Daniel take apart the remote, remove and hide the batteries, and remove the crayons from all the boxes and use them to build a fort, not to mention the toilet and the doorknob incidents. He had also noticed Daniel eyeing the back door leading to his work area in a disconcerting manner and had known it was only a matter of time until the miniature Houdini discovered a way to bypass the bell. He hadn't expected it to be as soon as today. "I'll see what I can come up with for the back door. It is very important that he not be able to wander outside while I've got machinery going."

Chloe barely suppressed a shiver of dread, "I'd just deadbolt it for the duration, but unfortunately, that's illegal."

He nodded and headed for the back door and a moment later disappeared from view.

The following day, Chloe noticed Deke get into his pickup and drive off at noon. He reappeared just as the kids were settled for naps. She heard him tap on the back door and opened it.

He smiled, "I'd like to introduce you to someone." He stepped back and only then did she see a woolly head peeking out the window of the truck parked beside the back door.

Intrigued, she stepped out of the doorway, "What's that?"

Deke opened his truck door and a dog the size of a small pony scrambled out. He ran in a circle around Deke, and then headed to check out Chloe.

"Heel," Deke's voice was firm, and immediately the animal halted and returned to Deke's side.

She smiled at the dog's goofy face and happy disposition, "What's his name? May I pet him?"

"Sure. Woofer, this is Chloe. Mind your manners." The dog's tail was going to make him airborne if he kept up the wagging. She reached out and scrubbed his head gently. His tongue snaked out swiftly, licking her wrist, but he didn't try to crowd her.

She smiled, "He's a sweetie. Hi, Woofer. The kids are going to love you."

Deke smiled in relief, "That's what I thought. I usually bring him with me to work sites, and he's been pouting for the past two days. So I told him I'd ask your permission to bring him from now on. He's obedience trained; he won't go anywhere without my permission, and he loves kids. If your helpers want, I brought a leash, and he'd be delighted to accompany them on any walks they take."

She nodded, secretly delighted he not only conversed with his dog but felt no embarrassment at relating their conversations with someone else. He was one seriously secure male. She gave Woofer one last hug then turned to go back in.

By four-thirty, there were only two children left, and as neither of them were Daniel, security could relax for the remainder of the day. At five the day care was empty, and she and Tasha were in the kitchen putting away the last of the dishes and washing down the counters.

They had agreed that Tasha would be paid for three hours of work each day whether kids left early or not. It didn't happen often and was a nice bonus for Tasha the days it did happen. She told Tasha to go home and watched her gather up her books and jump out the back door to the ground.

During the day, Deke had begun digging holes in the space where the new floor of the sun porch would go. The children crowded by the windows every moment they could to watch him. Within a few hours, he had the holes dug. When he had returned with Woofer, he also had the back end of the pickup filled with bags of concrete. While the kids napped, he mixed concrete in a wheelbarrow, using water from the hose, and filled the holes, setting pier blocks on top of each to hold the posts that would support the deck floor.

He stopped Tasha, and began grilling her, "I haven't seen the teenage delinquent appear yet. Did he come and leave without me seeing him?"

"Zach?" A frown marred her pretty face, "Why do you call him a delinquent? Because he's a skater? Skateboarding is not a crime, you know." She was not happy with this obtuse adult. "You're making a judgment based on his appearance."

He looked at her black turtleneck, jeans, and lace-up Doc Martens—almost a clone of Zach's outfit, albeit much more attractive on her—and caved. Laughing he held up his hands and backed away, "Uncle! Uncle! You're right. I'm making unwarranted assumptions. So, does he usually come home after school before he heads out to skateboard?"

"Oh, yeah," she nodded sagely, "he always comes home. He's a male teen, he needs food; lots of it. Most of the skaters are good guys though; at least the ones at the school are. I don't know if he knows any of the dropouts that are skaters, but some of them aren't such good guys."

"Hmm," he was curious as to why he cared; a more prickly kid he'd never seen. According to Tasha though, yesterday's exchange about breakfast had been an anomaly. He wondered if Chloe was worried about him after the words they'd exchanged. Maybe Zach had called her from school today and told her where he was headed. He thought about checking on her. Naw, the last thing she'd appreciate was him questioning Zach's non-appearance.

He finished just before six p.m. By then the light was fading, and he couldn't see clearly enough to continue. He neatly stacked all the lumber and loaded Woofer and his tools into the back of his truck. He hesitated, not sure whether or not to tell Chloe he was leaving. Noticing that all the lights were out on the ground floor, he decided it wasn't necessary. He climbed into his truck, turned a one-eighty in the yard, and headed down the driveway.

As he turned onto the street, Woofer gave a deep woof at a solitary figure of a skateboarder cruising up the sidewalk toward the front door. His headlights caught the

Mohawk silhouette as Zach looked up and called something to his dog. He was glad for Chloe's sake that her kid was home.

###

In the inexplicable volatile manner of adolescents, Zach was semi-chatty at supper. He helped her clear the table without any prompting, and then stood in the kitchen watching her with hopeful eyes.

She suppressed a smile, "Yes, Zach, get your jacket; we'll go to Northgate Mall and get your phone." There was an AT&T kiosk in the mall, and within the hour she and Zach had matching phones. She had upgraded hers while she was at it, with, to Zach's blissful delight, unlimited texting.

She went to bed at nine-thirty. She hesitated outside Zach's bedroom; it was so quiet inside she wondered if he was asleep, but a quiet knock elicited a "Yo!" so she cracked the door. As if. She rolled her eyes, no wonder it was quiet, he was stretched out on his bed texting. He lifted his head and waved his phone, "This is so cool, Mom. Ryan has the same plan so all our texts will be free."

She went to bed, ever hopeful that the zombies that had kidnapped her son had returned him today and they were over the worst of their relationship problems.

Chapter 6

Monday, Deke took the day off. She wondered, not for the first time, what he did on these mysterious days off. She was glad she had planned a field trip to the aquarium, as the kids were very disappointed that they couldn't look out the windows and see him working. She had planned the field trip to coincide with a teacher work day. Even knowing there would be more kids than usual at the aquarium because of a day off school, by planning it this way, she could count on Zach and Tasha coming along to help with the kids.

As always, they dressed everyone in over-sized, orange t-shirts lettered with The Perfect Child. At the site, they linked each child hand-in-hand with curly-wired hand guards (they were the most colorful chain gang anyone had seen) and assigned a group of four to each supervisor. As usual, Chloe made sure Daniel was in her team and the first one in line to hold her hand. He was such a darling. Watching his delight with the displays, she felt a surge of love for him.

He was unusually quiet at the shark tank, "Miss Chloe," he asked soberly, "do you think Mr. Deke's drill could go through this glass?" She felt fear frisson down her spine but consoled herself because there wasn't a power tool anywhere around.

"Remember how thick the guide said the glass is?"

He nodded, "One-foot thick."

"I don't think Mr. Deke has a drill bit that is

twelve inches long, Daniel."

"Oh," with a last longing look at the display he allowed her to lead her brood away.

She had packed a picnic lunch, and after the aquarium, they walked two blocks to Waterfront Park and ate their meal on the grass overlooking the water. At lunch, clutching his sandwich in one hand, it was obvious Daniel was still giving the breech of the shark cage his full attention. "How about if Mr. Deke glued two bits together? Would that be long enough to go through the shark's glass?"

Zach overheard and joined her in assuring Daniel that drilling through the glass wall was not a good idea and then diverted him by pointing out two seagulls fighting over a piece of bread.

Most days Chloe found herself walking outside in the afternoon to observe what had been accomplished. It usually resulted in her and Deke sparring, and she refused to admit that their interchanges stirred her blood. He made her feel more alive than she had in over a year, and she found it both exciting and frightening. She didn't think she was imagining Deke's enjoyment over their talks each day.

Today, she eyed the framework of a wall that Deke had erected and braced with splayed two-by-fours.

"Does that stud look straight to you?" She squinted at it.

He shook his head in mock exasperation, "You are a piece of work. Yes, it does look straight." He took a break to grab a cup of coffee from his thermos.

She grinned and took a swallow of her own coffee, "Just checking."

Deke sighed in resignation, a hint of a smile in his eyes. "Where's skate-boy today?" he queried.

"It's only three o'clock. School is barely out. He'll be here."

She barely had the words out before Zach trudged up the drive.

Chloe saw him eye her son, again glimpsing something sad in his gaze. He hesitated before saying, "Hey, Zach."

"Hi," Zach quickly straightened his shoulders and went past them toward the back door.

"Hi, son," Chloe's bright greeting belied the concern evident in her gaze. Zach gave a grunt, never turning his head as he entered the kitchen. The pain in her body language made Deke feel his observation was an intrusion.

"I'm sorry," his eyes were serious. She turned away, rejecting the kindness she saw there. Fighting with him was easier to handle than his sympathy.

"Is something bothering Zach? He seemed worried about something."

"I wouldn't know. My son doesn't talk to me."

"Not talking to parents is apparently what teens do best."

"Maybe, but something is wrong with him, I'm sure of it; I just don't know what."

"Is there an adult he would talk to? Maybe his youth pastor?"

"There's no one. He doesn't like the youth group at church; he won't even try to make friends there. He went one time and said they were stuck up yuppies-in-the-making and he met enough of that type at Fowler. He goes willingly to the regular services with me; he just isn't interested in their youth group."

She suddenly curled in on herself, vulnerable, "You'd think that if God had to take one of us, that he would have taken Zach's mother and left him the father he so desperately needs to grow into a well-rounded adult male."

"Don't ever say that," he muttered, surprised at the emotion rising in him, when he barely knew Chloe, "God doesn't make mistakes." He saw her mouth open in hot response and plowed on, "I know. It appears to us that He makes a lot of mistakes, but one thing I had to settle when I was born again and trying to make sense of my lousy life, was the truth that God doesn't make mistakes. Plus, He takes the mistakes we make and uses them to help us grow."

He could tell it didn't seem to be helping, but he felt impelled to keep going, "Anyway, everyone insists what kids need most is time and attention by their parents." He clamped his mouth shut remembering Chloe's busy schedule. *Great, Deke, make her feel even more guilty. Why don't you just stomp her?*

She stared blindly at the house and then shook her head. "You're right. He's been alone too much. I've been getting the business going and continuing my former life. It hasn't been wise to leave Zach alone three nights a week. I forgot that it hadn't mattered before, because when I was gone, he and Phillip were together doing guy stuff."

Curious, he asked, "What was it you did in this former life?"

"I volunteered. It's a legacy from my mother. Volunteering is programmed into my DNA, but the other night, Zach mentioned that he hated coming home to a dark house. It was the first honest feeling he's expressed since we moved here, so you can be sure I am in the process of trying to hand off my commitments. I am not ignoring this."

"That's very wise of you. You have my admiration, if it's worth anything." A thought struck him, "If volunteering is coded into your DNA, how about choosing somewhere Zach could join you? I volunteer over at the soup kitchen on Fourth Ave. I've been there for over a year, and they always need help." He grimaced, "Except holidays. I know it's wrong to knock social consciousness, but when it is only activated twice a year—Thanksgiving and Christmas—it's hard not to be cynical."

"Hmm, that's a good idea. What do you do there?"

"I help serve Thursday supper then stay and hold a Bible study. We're studying Colossians."

She gazed into the distance, "I guess we get into ruts. And once we're involved with something, we realize how big a hole we'll leave if we quit. Since there wouldn't be anything for Zach at a crisis pregnancy center, maybe it's time for a change for me."

"Crisis pregnancy center?" He tried not to let the frisson of chill that ran up his spine show. "What do you do there?"

"I mostly do administrative stuff. I can fill in on the hotline if needed, but my main love is coordinating the PAS classes."

"PAS? What does that stand for?"

"Post Abortion Syndrome."

He spewed his coffee, "Oh come on! You're making that up."

She eyed him steadily, "No, it's a very real after-affect that Planned Parenthood doesn't want their clients to know about. They tell a girl that getting rid of a fetus is all that matters and that once it's gone, all her problems will be over. Not true."

He couldn't move. Not if his life depended on it. His heart was pounding and there was a roaring in his ears. Instantly, he was pulled back to being seventeen years old and standing outside the abortion clinic in Mobile. He could see the building as clearly as if it was yesterday. He had driven his fifteen-year-old girlfriend there that hot, Saturday afternoon. He still relived that day in his nightmares—the dirt, the buzzing flies, the scent of medication that permeated the building. He hadn't gone inside with her; he had sat in the car alone.

Several hours had crept by before the passenger door opened and Belinda slid onto the seat. She hadn't spoken a word; she hadn't looked at him. She just stared through the windshield on the drive home. They hadn't discussed anything about what had happened and before the summer ended they had broken up. When he turned eighteen, he enlisted in the Army. For what they had been told was such a non-incident, he still remembered every single detail.

And before he had accepted Christ, each time he had gotten drunk, he had relived that afternoon, wondering if he would have been a father to a son or a daughter had always driven him to start a fight in an effort to erase the agony that thrummed deep inside.

He became aware that she was touching his arm, and her eyes were concerned. She was saying something, and he forced a response, "What?"

"Are you okay?" Her green eyes were full of concern. "You seemed to go somewhere, and I wondered if I had said something wrong."

He took a tighter grip on himself, "No, no, I'm fine. Just got to thinking about some old incident. Sorry I drifted off."

She nodded, but her eyes were full of compassion, an emotion he knew would disappear in a heartbeat if he had blurted out his story.

He took a firm grip on his emotions and forced his mind back to their original conversation, "What church do you go to?"

"Queen Anne Covenant. When we moved here I saw advertisements for it and thought it would be a help to Zach."

"Why?"

She stared at him nonplussed, "Why? Well, because a youth group is a very important peer group for teens."

He swirled the coffee in the bottom of his cup, watching it as if it held the answer to the mysteries of the universe. "So, you knew these kids and felt satisfied that they would be the best influence on Zach as possible?"

"No, of course I didn't know them," her exasperation leeched out, because to be honest, she still didn't know them. Almost six months later, she wasn't acquainted with any of their parents, either. This church was nothing like the one they'd been involved in when they lived in San Diego. There, they had served on committees, hosted a small group in their home, and served as advisors on the middle school board in anticipation for the day Zach would be old enough to join that group.

He shifted to lean against a pile of lumber stacked next to the house, "Have you ever considered that maybe what Zach needs is a whole church he can relate to? An entire congregation who loves him and is interested in investing in his life?"

"Where would I find that in Seattle? Your description sounds more like a small-town church, like the church my grandpa pastored." Her Grandpa McKinnon had died before she was born, but her Grammy still lived in Emmett, Idaho, where he had pastored the Emmett Community Church for over forty years. Her mom had been raised in the parsonage there, and the stories she told had seemed like something out of the Little House on the Prairie series.

He watched her smile as she remembered something good. "Last time Zach and I visited was my cousin Miranda's wedding on New Year's Day. We had a wonderful time. She married the current pastor of the church that Grandpa McKinnon pastored. Now, she and Joel and their family lived in the downstairs of the old parsonage, while Grammy and Uncle Robert, mom's oldest brother, lived on the second floor."

"Wow," Deke was impressed. He couldn't imagine what it would be like to have a heritage like hers, "You and Zach are really blessed, Chloe."

"I know," she was still gazing at a distant picture.

She tuned back to Deke's conversation and what he was saying, "Well, maybe Queen Anne Covenant doesn't have what Zach needs. Ever since I was born again, I've attended medium to small churches." He shifted to face her, his eyes serious, "Because I never had a family growing up, I know the value of one and what it contributes to emotional wholeness; no matter where I've lived, I've always found those attributes in small churches.

"At All Souls Community Parish, we aren't large

enough to afford the salary for a youth pastor. The parents take turns leading group meetings, and everyone pitches in on game and activity nights. There are always a whole host of interested people of all ages wanting to connect with the teens, and our kids thrive on the commitment we have to them. They're not perfect, and often," he grinned remembering something, "when one of them screws up, they know they're going to be running a whole gamut of reactions from the adults the next time they see them."

He took a deep breath and took the plunge, "As a matter of fact, we're having a chili supper and volleyball night this Friday. How about you and Zach coming to it with me? You can meet a few people and decide for yourself if it would be a good fit for Zach."

What did she have to lose? "I'd like that, but how about if you invite Zach yourself? He seems to resent anything I've planned lately."

"You got it."

Much to her surprise, when Zach appeared in the kitchen precisely on time that night and took a chair at the dinner table, he actually conversed with her in more than grunts. Having him in such an amiable mood, she wondered if she should set any ground work for Deke's invitation, but decided to leave well enough alone.

Going to bed she felt hope rise again that they were going to be fine. Why had she ever been glad she was raising a boy instead of a girl? It appeared that adolescent males weren't any easier to raise than females – hormones wreaked the same havoc on both sexes.

Chapter 7

The next day, Chloe was outside surveying the work and sparring with Deke when Tasha and Zach arrived after school together. Chloe and Deke were both laughing at something, and as Zach approached, he glowered at Deke, “Aren’t you supposed to be working, not flirting with my mother?”

Shocked, Chloe gasped, but Deke didn’t hesitate. He took two steps so he and Zach were face to face, “You apologize to your mother right now. That was out of line.”

Zach, in the way of teens whose mouths have overrun their common sense, was overcome with embarrassment, turned beet red, and muttered, “Sorry, Mom.”

She recovered her breath, almost in tears over her son’s behavior, “Apology accepted. You also need to apologize to Deke. You have no right to speak to an adult in that manner. I raised you better than that, and I expect you to remember it.”

Zach’s head hung even lower, but he again muttered, “I’m sorry,” to Deke.

Chloe wasn’t done with him, “Look him in the eye, and say it in a voice we can both hear.”

Zach swallowed, lifted his head, and repeated, “I’m sorry,” his eyes on Deke’s face, but not meeting his glance.

Deke nodded, “Thank you. Apology accepted.”

Chloe was on a tear, "You will help with the kids after school for a week without pay. And for today, you are grounded from your skateboard? Am I clear?" Zach nodded and escaped into the house, slamming the door behind him.

Tasha broke the silence, "Kids," she sighed. Deke and Chloe turned to look at her. Tasha nodded like a miniature adult, today's bright blue hair reminiscent of a trendy little old lady. Deke and Chloe turned to gaze at each other for a moment then burst into laughter as she turned to go inside.

Alone again, Chloe discovered she was still too embarrassed to meet Deke's eyes herself. Finally, she sighed, shrugged, and looked at him, "What can I say? My son is impossible, and I'm a failure."

Deke smiled, "No, teens are just difficult. Remember Dr. Dobson's advice for dealing with a teen?"

"No," she'd often listened to Focus on the Family, especially when Zach was younger, but didn't recall this particular piece of advice.

"He said when a teen hits puberty you should put them in a barrel and feed them through a hole."

She grinned, "Sounds tempting."

"And when they hit fifteen…plug the hole."

He was glad to see the smile morph into a chuckle.

Deke faced her, "Seriously, males are pretty headstrong. Without an alpha male around to keep them in line, they keep pushing until they find where the boundaries lie." He looked at her, "I guess today may not be a good time to invite him to the chili feed. Maybe tomorrow."

She was silent for a while, digesting his seemingly

innocent comment. "Do you think I let Zach get away with things?" she asked after a moment.

He stopped what he was doing and looked at her soberly, "I know you let Zach get away with things. Are you sure you want to start this conversation?"

She wrapped her arms around her middle, feeling vulnerable, but knowing she needed to hear Deke's opinion. For some reason it seemed important to her. "You mean because I think he should be free to express his feelings?"

He shook his head, "No, because you haven't taught him that nobody gets to say anything they wish." He shoved his hammer into a ring on his tool belt. "The really puzzling thing to me is that I don't believe that is normal behavior for you. Were you this lenient when your husband was alive?"

Bingo! She felt her face flush, "What are you saying? You think I'm compensating because my kid lost his father?" Her mouth twisted as she registered her words, and she sighed, "Yeah, you're right. He never got away with the stuff he does now."

Her eyes, now defenseless, met Deke's, "When he was younger, I knew what was best for him. It's a whole new ballgame having a teenager and raising him on my own. I feel I'm paddling my canoe in the middle of a river headed for the falls."

He took a moment to analyze her words, before responding, "Chloe, I know parenting has to change as kids get older, but he's only thirteen, not eighteen. Your fear that you can't do a good job as a single parent is just a lie of the Enemy's. God knew you would be doing this alone, and He is willing to fill in the gaps for you if you'll rely on Him, not your fears. The only people better at manipulation than toddlers are teens, and Zach is playing you like a violin."

She nodded, "I know you're right, I just don't know where to start."

He reached out and laid his hand over hers, "I will pray for wisdom for you. I believe you when you say that Zach is a good kid. I hope you'll make the necessary changes soon; you don't want to lose him. Believe me when I say that the streets are no place to grow up."

She didn't respond but turned back toward the house.

He watched her disappear and reflected on his last words. He was aware that he had lied, because he really didn't think Zach was a good kid – the teen was secretive and way too rebellious. He hoped for Chloe's sake that she was right and he was wrong.

The next afternoon, Deke was alone in the back when Zach appeared around the corner of the house.

"Hi, Zach," Deke took care to glance at him casually. "Would you mind grabbing the other end of this tape and stringing it down that wall?" He extended the end of his fifty-foot metal tape to the teen. Zach shrugged out of his backpack and dropped his skateboard. "Okay," he grabbed it, unrolling the tape as he moved down the side of the addition, "where do you need it?"

"Just put the lip of it over the outer edge." Zach followed his instructions, and Deke made note of the measurement. "Now, let's do it from the house," Zach picked up the end and moved down the length.

"Great, thanks, that's what I needed," Deke flipped up the tape and allowed it to coil back into his hand, making a rattling sound as it rewound. "Do you like to work with your hands?" he inquired casually.

"I don't know," Zach said softly. "The only thing I can remember making with my dad was my Pinewood Derby car for Awanas. Then dad got sick, and we didn't do much like that anymore." He firmed his shoulders and looked at him, "I bet we would have; he used to talk about what we were going to do when he got better. He used to talk about us building a tree house together at first, but after a while he didn't bring it up anymore."

"I'm sorry, that sucks," there was no mistaking Deke's sincerity.

"Yeah, well, stuff happens."

"I never knew my dad; mostly I picked my skills up working on construction crews when I got out of the Army."

"I've often thought it would be cool to know how to build a bookcase or something," Deke hoped that Zach didn't realize how wistful he sounded.

"Yeah? I have built some furniture, and it is cool." He decided to take the window that had presented itself, "I see you're good at skateboarding, do you like any other sports?"

"Well, not football." Zach grimaced, "Thank goodness Fowler doesn't have it in their athletic program."

Deke laughed, "Okay, what ones do you like?"

"Well, skateboarding," he grinned and Deke could see his mom in the urchin smile. "Fowler has fencing for the upper classmen, and I plan to take that when I'm a junior."

"Sounds cool. Ever play volleyball?"

"My youth group in San Diego played it all the time at the beach. It's fun."

"Yeah? Well, the church I go to is small, so when we have a social and play volleyball, everyone plays, from Bessie Fetter, who is sixty-five and has a wicked serve, to nine-year-old Benjamin. And as it happens, this Friday is our quarterly church social. We're having chili dogs, homemade ice cream, and a volleyball marathon. Would you and your mom like to go with me? Maybe meet some new friends? You could ask Tasha to come too if you'd like."

He held his breath while Zach analyzed the invitation from every angle, looking for hidden danger. Finally he cautiously agreed, "Well, it sounds okay. It's not like we do anything anyway on Friday nights." He thought, "Maybe I'll go talk to mom and Tasha and see what they think."

"Let me know. I think you'd have a good time."

In much less time than he expected, Zach came bounding back out, "Yeah, we'd like to go. Tasha says she'll just stay after work and ride with us. Mom wants to know what she should bring and what time and where," he took a deep breath and gulped down half the can of 7-Up in his hand.

"It's at six-thirty. She doesn't need to bring anything; you're my guests. I will swing by and pick all of you up this time since you don't know where we're going."

Zach eyed his pickup dubiously, "We won't all fit in your Chevy."

"Well," Deke drawled, "lucky for me I have a Jeep huh?"

Zach grinned. "Okay I'll tell them to be ready. Guess I'd better get back in there; I'm on Daniel detail until he goes home."

###

At six-thirty on the dot Friday evening, Deke pulled up to the back of the house in a black Jeep Cherokee. He held the door for Chloe as she slid onto the cream leather passenger seat. Tasha and Zach climbed into the back and fastened their seatbelts. Without examining his reasons too carefully, only knowing that he felt safer having more people in the party than two kids, he had tried his best to talk Mrs. Watanabe into going along, but she had refused. With everyone buckled up, he turned down Queen Anne, merging onto Deshler and crossed the Fremont Bridge. The eighteen-foot Fremont Troll, a popular landmark, was not visible from the top since he actually resided under the nearby Aurora Bridge. He crossed over several side streets and in a few minutes pulled into the parking lot of his church. The lot was already filling up, and friendly hellos were exchanged as they exited his vehicle. Opening the back of the Jeep, he unloaded the Crockpot of chili that had been simmering on his counter all day, and they walked toward the gymnasium at the back.

Inside it was a jumble of laughter and talk, mixed with the fragrant smells of chili simmering on the stove. A whiff of chocolate, probably the dessert, ruffled along the edges of their senses. The kitchen crew was just getting ready to serve, and Pastor Markham called for heads to be bowed while he prayed over the meal and for the safety of those facing Bessie Fetter's serve. Chloe experienced déjà vu in the laughter and hum of friendly conversation, realizing this already felt more like home to her than Queen Anne ever had.

Standing in line, Deke was suddenly aware that he and Chloe were alone. He looked around, searching for Zach and Tasha, and spotted them speaking to a couple of teens who had just entered the gym. Then he remembered that the Olsen twins, a boy and a girl, attended Fowler Academy themselves. Their parents had shared the good news at their passing the rigorous entrance exams last spring.

"Looks like there's someone here that Tasha and Zach know," he nodded his head toward the foursome.

She observed them for a moment, "They seem like nice kids. It would be really great if Zach found someone to be friends with. Who knows, maybe this time I'll get an introduction."

As if on cue, the quartet moved their way. It was Tasha who made the introductions, "Chloe, this is Angela and Andrew Olsen; they go to Fowler with us. We thought the four of us would eat together. Will that be okay?"

Chloe smiled and extended her hand to the teens to shake, "I'm glad to meet you. Are you in Tasha's classes?"

"No," Andrew responded, "we're in Zach's grade. I have Zach in Algebra, and Angela has him in World History." Zach nodded in agreement.

"Well, you guys go do your thing. We'll be fine." She made a shooing motion with her hand, and the four took off for the end of the line. She continued to watch them, seeing that Zach was the most animated he'd been since moving to Seattle. Well, except for the aberration of excitement when she'd bought him the cell phone. She turned her head to catch Deke's gaze on her.

"Well?" he lifted an eyebrow.

She took a deep breath and released it, "Thank you very much. This is the most connected I've seen my son since leaving California. I am in debt to you."

"So can I expect no more nagging?"

She grinned, unaware of the dimple that appeared in the corner of her mouth, "Don't be silly."

He eyed her for a moment then shook his head as if to wake up, "Didn't think so."

They were at the head of the line now. He handed her a plate, bowl, and silverware. All she wanted was a bowl of chili and crackers, while he ordered three chili dogs to the jeers of the kitchen crew.

One of the servers asked, "Do you want to try Deke's chili?"

"Sure, which one is yours?"

He indicated his Crockpot, and she watched the woman ladle a generous amount into her bowl. She leaned down to inhale the fragrance, "Mmm, smells delicious. Do you have any secret ingredients?"

"Just venison," he watched her closely to see if she would freak.

"Great," she beamed, following him to one of the tables, "I love venison. Elk is my favorite wild meat, but venison is good." And it was. It was delicious. "You're a great cook," she commented, scraping the bottom of her bowl.

"I don't know about great, but I like to putter in the kitchen. I quickly tired of packaged or fast food, so I bought a couple of cookbooks and began to learn. Now the Food Network is one of my vices."

"Mine too! Which show do you like best?"

"Anything with Alton Brown is good. Tyler is also great."

She nodded, "I prefer Giada. Her recipes are easy and quick."

She felt comfortable talking to him. He carried his

part of the conversation and had great manners. Each time people joined their table he introduced Chloe as a friend he was working for. She found everyone to be warm and friendly. Each time she glanced around for Zach she found him sitting with the same group of kids and appearing to be having a great time himself. She realized that this was the first time since they had moved to Seattle that she didn't have a knot in her stomach. It felt great to relax and enjoy herself.

After about an hour of dining, by some unseen command, everyone began to rise, clear tables, and fold up chairs. In a matter of minutes the floor was cleared, and a volleyball net was stretched across the middle.

The first game matched those under twenty-one against those over. The overs won the first game but lost the next two. Chloe felt long-unused muscles protest as she stretched to return serves and laughed at the various calamities that always occur with amateurs. At one point, Deke reached out to return a volley headed straight toward her head, and she put her shoulder into his side to move him out of her way. At she sent it soaring over the net she warned, "Stay out of my way, Hudson," and he rubbed his side and grinned good-naturedly.

The over-twenties ran out of energy after the third game, and the call went out for boys against girls. Chloe sat it out, but Deke joined the boys' team for one game and then came to collapse next to her.

To her surprise it was almost eleven before they left. The car was quiet on the way home. They dropped Tasha off first then Deke pulled into their back lot for Zach and Chloe to disembark.

Without any prompting, Zach said, "Thanks, man. I had fun tonight. I'm glad I went."

Deke smiled at him, "I'm glad you did too. It's

great you found some friends there. Maybe you'll consider coming back some time."

Zach nodded, "Andrew told me about the youth group. I'm going to talk to Mom about it."

He moved on into the house, and Chloe turned to look up at Deke. She took a deep breath, "Thank you so very much for tonight. I'm more hopeful about my son right now than I have been since we moved. If he wishes to attend your youth group, we're changing churches. Finding one he enjoys attending it too important."

He smiled down at her, "I'm glad it went well. Thank you for coming with me."

They both paused, looking into each other's eyes almost without breathing, but then Zach flipped on the kitchen light, and the moment was gone. With a bemused smile, Chloe entered the house.

Chapter 8

By mid afternoon the following Tuesday, Deke stopped work to assess how well the job was progressing and felt a sense of satisfaction at what he had done. He was aware of a sense of restlessness, and since it was that true rarity in Seattle—a sunny afternoon—on an impulse he loaded his tools and headed home. He had been avoiding Chloe since the chili feed and was aware she was doing the same – she hadn't come out either yesterday or today to banter with him. He wasn't sure where their relationship was headed, not sure if it could even be called a relationship, and he needed a ride.

He swung by home, parked his Chevy, unloaded Woofer, and climbed on his Harley. He didn't waste any time unloading his truck; it would all still be there when he returned, but the sun might not last long. He pulled onto the interstate and revved up the engine, relaxing in direct proportion to his speed as he raced north on the freeway. Forty minutes later, at Everett, he left the interstate and swung through the countryside on side roads, enjoying the glimpses of Mount Baker through the trees and the soothing scenery, a delightful proximity to the big city that surprised so many visitors. Cows in the field eyed him as he roared past, horses galloped alongside him on their side of the fence as far as their paddock allowed. Geese in a few yards strutted and fluttered their wings, warning him against bringing that noisy contraption into their domain.

Inevitably his thoughts came around to Chloe and

Zach. He felt sadness at the problems they were having and wished he could solve them. But he reminded himself that problem solving was a specialty of God's. As he rolled along he prayed, "Help Chloe see the damage she is doing to her son. Give her hope for the future and wisdom for the steps she needs to take. Comfort her in her grief and show her that you are with her every step of the way. And God, talk to Zach. Remind him that you will never leave him, even when people are taken away, you are never gone, and he always has you to talk to."

He realized as he returned home almost ninety minutes later that he felt much lighter than he had in several days.

It was past six o'clock when he rode up his street and pulled into his drive. As he accelerated past the end of the house, a group of teens milling in the space between his house and garage scattered like ants. It was evident the teens had ignored the No Trespassing signs and had come back. He brought the bike to a halt, kicked it onto its stand, and looked around to see what they might have been doing; immediately the smell of smoke assailed him, and adrenalin flooded his system. Fire was the worst possible scenario given all the wood and glue products he had. His head turned toward his workshop, terror coursing through his veins, but he quickly became aware that the smell came from the blackberry thicket.

He broke into a run, pushing through the vines to reach the clearing. At the site of the hideout, there was one lone figure fighting a small blaze. He paid scant attention to the kid, but noted he was at least attempting to control the fire by kicking dirt on the flames. Realizing they didn't have much time before it would get out of hand, he turned and ran back to the tool shed approximately fifty feet away. Thanking whatever instinct had made him buy a hundred-foot hose, he grabbed the nozzle, wrenched open the spigot, and dragged it to the blaze.

"Stand back," he barked at the figure still scooping up dirt to kill the flames, and startled, the kid jumped back. Deke aimed the water on the fire and within a few minutes it was completely out. Only then did he turn toward the teenager who, much to his surprise, had not fled when he approached.

"What do you think you were doing?" he bellowed. "Do you know how much wood I have around here? You kids could have destroyed my whole business. What were you thinking to build a fire?"

The figure turned to face him, bravely, and his jaw sagged. "Zach?" At some point water and sweat had plastered the Mohawk to his skull, and he hadn't recognized him. "What are you trying to do? Did you know this was my property?"

He shook his head, "We always came in the back way. We thought the property was abandoned."

"So that gave you the right to try to burn it down?"

"No," Zach lifted his chin bravely, "we weren't trying to burn it down." His eyes dropped to the ground, and he muttered, "One of the guys was smoking, and he didn't make sure the butt was totally out before he dropped it. Before we knew it the weeds caught fire, then they jumped to a pile of brush, and everyone panicked. I think some of them went to find a bucket or something, but when you arrived, they ran."

Deke eyed him in silence. His eyes sharpened as he looked down at Zach's hands, he was holding stiffly away from his clothing. He blew out a breath. Now was not the time to kill the kid.

"Let me see your hands, son," he said quietly.

"They're fine," Zach snatched them behind his back.

"No, you've burned them haven't you?"

"They're fine." His outthrust chin was reminiscent of a certain redhead's jaw when she was defensive.

Deke stepped toward the path, "Come on, I'll take you home and let your mom tend to your hands. We need to talk anyway." In silence, Zach followed him out of the clearing. Deke motioned him toward the pickup, parked up by the shed; they climbed into the cab, Deke turned over the engine, and they headed to The Perfect Child day care.

Chloe had evidently been watching for Zach, for she had the downstairs door open by the time they drove up, "Deke? Zach?" her arms were wrapped around her middle, "What happened?" By this time, they stood in the glow of the porch light, and she could smell the smoke and see soot on Zach's clothing and skin, "Zacheus, what happened to you?" Her eyes darted between her son and Deke.

Behind him, Deke urged Zach forward with a hand on his shoulder. "He appears to have some first and second degree burns on his hands, Mom. Let's get him cleaned up and see if he needs a doctor. Then we can talk."

Chloe didn't say anything more; she simply turned and headed upstairs to their apartment, Zach and Deke following. Pushing her son down on the commode, she inspected his hands, asked if he had any other burns, and when he shook his head, opened the medicine cabinet and proceeded to clean and bind his wounds. She shook her head a couple of times, but other than that didn't voice any of her concerns. When she had thrown away the detritus of medical care, she turned to Deke and folded her arms, "Okay, tell me what this is about."

"I think he needs something to drink or he might black out on you," Deke said quietly, indicating Zach huddled by the side of the sink.

She turned and her expression softened, "Come on, son, let's get something in you."

Leading the way to the kitchen, she opened the refrigerator door while Deke pulled out a chair at the table and guided Zach to it. Behind him, Chloe popped the top of a can of cola and handed it to Zach. She turned the oven off on what smelled like a delicious meal and stuck two pieces of bread in the toaster. When they popped up, she spread peanut butter and honey on them, put them together into a sandwich, and handed it to Zach, "Can you hold this or should I break it up into small pieces?"

Zach shook his head, "I can hold it," and he did okay, using the tips of his fingers to guide it to his mouth. The sandwich provided much needed protein, and his color returned in a few minutes.

While Zach was eating, Chloe reopened the oven door and began to dish up the supper.

Keeping a close eye on her son, she asked Deke, "Do you mind grabbing three plates from that cupboard?" She indicated which one with her head, "And the silverware's in that drawer," another nod directed him.

In bemusement he set the table, poured coffee for her and himself, and then waited until she was seated before taking his place at the table. She bowed her head, said grace, and added, "And thank you God for keeping Zach safe tonight and sending Deke to help him. You are so good to us, and we praise your name for your watchful eye." She finished and began passing food. Fragrant roast, brown gravy, mashed potatoes, sweet garden peas, and a fruit salad disappeared down three mouths without any conversation. In less than half an hour all the food was gone, the table was cleared, and Deke was glad to see that Zach had lost his green appearance.

Then Chloe refilled their cups with coffee, scooted her chair back, and began pacing, "What happened? One of you had better tell me right now." She was like a demented little bumper car ricocheting from cabinet to table to fridge.

Deke waited and was glad to see Zach sit up straight and speak, "Some of us guys built a fort in the back of Deke's property. Only we didn't know it was Deke's land; we thought it was abandoned. We've been hanging out there sometimes, just talking and stuff.

"Only today," he sighed, facing plans that had gone wrong, "some of the older guys who hang out at the park followed us there. They liked what we'd built and decided it was going to be theirs. In fact, they went and found the tarp that had been taken down and stretched it back out. We didn't know what to do; they are bigger and older and meaner. Before we could decide, we heard Deke's bike come roaring up the driveway and everyone scattered." He took a breath and continued, "One of the guys was smoking and flicked his cigarette away without dousing it, and it began a small fire. I was trying to put it out when Deke grabbed the hose and finished."

If it had been a humorous situation, Deke would have been amused to see what it was that could finally render Chloe speechless. Since she appeared unable to find words, he decided he'd better say his piece, as he was sure that once she did start to speak, no one would be saying anything for awhile.

"It appears to have done minimal damage; however, it is vandalism. I can go to the police about it," he ignored Zach's horrified gasp, "or I can make Zach responsible for paying it back. Whichever you wish."

Zach bounced to his feet outraged, "What? I wasn't the one smoking. I stayed and tried to put out the blaze." His voice registered indignation at Deke's reaction to his Good Samaritan deed.

Chloe found her voice and locked onto her son like a missile, "You were trespassing. That is a criminal offence. Anything that happens in the commission of a crime becomes the fault of everyone involved, whether they did the actual deed or not. You definitely are to blame."

Zach deflated, but she wasn't done, and in spite of what Deke considered her shortcomings, she impressed him now.

Pinning Zach with a glare she said, "I should allow him to call the police and let you deal with them. However, if you can convince him of some way you can pay back the damage done to his property, I will allow it this time. Zacheus Phillip Evans you know better than to go anywhere or take or use anything that does not belong to you. You told me you were at the skate park every afternoon. Now that I know you were not, now that I know I cannot trust your word, things are definitely going to be different. For the foreseeable future, you are grounded young man. Not only that, I want to know every single kid you spend any time with, and if you're not willing to bring them home and introduce them to me, you don't have any friends. Now I suggest you begin talking to Deke and see what can be worked out."

Having said her piece, she marched to the sink where she proceeded to clear away the remains of the very delicious dinner they had enjoyed, banging silverware and slamming metal pans. Deke feared for the dishes.

Yup, she can be a force of nature when she lets herself go. He sat, waiting for the surly teen, staring at his feet as if hoping they would carry him way, to make the first move. Zach was obviously feeling very ill-used for staying to fight the fire.

Deke understood his feelings; to the kid's way of thinking, he was being punished for doing right. Unfortunately, that would be the acceptable reasoning to almost every one of his peers. He needed a reality check in the worst of ways. It was more than time for him to learn that remorse over a wrong didn't absolve it.

Finally the teen spoke to Deke, addressing his shoulder, "Is there some way I could work off the cost of the damages?" The words were forced out in a growl.

Deke stifled a groan. The last thing he wanted was to have this hood hanging around with his attitude, but he had started it by bringing him home instead of calling the police. Evidently God believed there was something he could do. Against his better judgment, he nodded, "I could use a good helper after school at the work site. Do you know anything about carpentry?"

"Nope," Zach hunched his shoulders, believing he'd lost his chance at restitution.

"Well, then, guess I'll teach you." At his hopeful gaze, Deke added, "A lot of it will be grunt work—don't kid yourself—but if you like it, I'll teach you something about construction too." He paused, "Just looking at the site, the only damage I could see was to that tarp that was burned. Canvas tarps are expensive, that one was probably a hundred and fifty dollars."

"A hundred and fifty dollars!" Zach's eyes bulged, "No way!"

Deke nodded, "Construction materials don't come cheap, and I buy the best so they'll last a long time. I figure a go-fer is worth ten bucks an hour, so you owe me fifteen hours of work."

Zach slumped in his chair then nodded okay. He turned to his mom, "Can I go now?"

She turned from the sink and eyed him for a moment, then crossed to a cabinet. She took down a bottle, shook two capsules into her hand, and handed them to Zach with a glass of water. Her voice was gentle, "Swallow these and go climb into bed. Don't even shower tonight since you can't get your hands wet. I'll wrap them in plastic tomorrow morning. If you wake up during the night in pain, come get me, and I'll get you more pain pills." She leaned forward and placed a kiss on his forehead, "Get some sleep son;, it'll look better in the morning."

As he turned, Deke spoke, "By the way, I didn't say it earlier and I should have, thank you for saving my property. It was a very brave and mature action to stay and not run like the others."

Zach eyed him and his mom for a moment then nodded and headed to bed.

As the door closed, Chloe sighed and collapsed into a chair. "I don't know what to do," she muttered, burying her head in her hands. She straightened and leaned back, closing her eyes, "I guess moving here was a really bad idea. I've really screwed up with my son."

He shifted and his tone changed, "I know how worried you are about your cub and his skateboarding every chance he gets, but you're really wondering what else he might be doing, aren't you?" She didn't answer and he continued, "It doesn't appear that he has any other interest beyond skateboarding. How about tempting him with a new one? One he could do at home. I don't know if he has any interest in carpentry, but I guess we'll find out in the next week or so. Maybe if he does then after he's done working for me he could build something for himself—a bookcase or a skateboard.

"If his love of skateboarding is genuine, you might allow him to build a skate ramp out back and invite his friends to skate here. You have quite a bit of property, and I think one would fit between the garage and shed just fine. Your day care charges would be contained in the yard once it's re-fenced, but they could still enjoy watching the older kids skateboard."

She could mentally see everything he was describing, then reality hit, and she sighed, "I don't have enough money to hire someone to build a skateboard ramp, I'm using the last of my capital from the sale of our home in California to finance this remodel."

In for a penny, in for a pound, Deke told himself grimly and forced the next words out of his mouth, "Hire someone? I didn't say to hire someone. If he'd like to try building a skateboard, the materials won't be expensive. I've probably got most of them at my place, left over from other jobs. Zach appears to have the concentration necessary for a detailed project; I've seen him working with the kids, and he's pretty good. The skate ramp is a big project for later. Let's just play this by ear for now."

She eyed him warily, "Why would you offer to help him? He's been nothing but rude to you."

He shrugged, paused for a moment then answered honestly, "Maybe I see myself in him at that age. Maybe I believe you when you tell me he's really a good kid who's having a rough time. I don't know. Think about it at any rate. He needs something constructive to do with his time."

There didn't seem to be anything more to say, so after a few minutes, Deke thanked Chloe for supper and rose to leave.

She walked him to the door of the apartment, and Deke paused with one hand on the knob looking down at her. He considered kissing her just to get the anticipation over with. Maybe there wouldn't be any chemistry and this attraction would come to nothing. But tonight was not the time to find out. She was exhausted, and if and when he kissed her, he wanted her undivided attention, not half of it on her cub.

Someday, he ruminated on his way to his truck, they needed to discuss their attraction to each other. Unfortunately, kid situations seem to interfere with the normal man/woman interaction. He'd be the first to state that dating a mother was a lot harder than he had anticipated, except he couldn't feel anything he and Chloe had done could qualify as dating.

Chapter 9

If pressed, Deke would've admitted he was surprised when Zach appeared in the backyard promptly at three o'clock the next afternoon.

"Okay, I'm here. What's first?" The *I don't give a rip* bravado in his voice was belied by his stance.

Deke didn't respond to the words; the kid was barely a hundred pounds of misery. His own memories of being thirteen and the smallest in the class rose up and knotted his throat. Judging by the size of those feet—why did he even need a skateboard? Just slip wheels beneath his tennis shoes, and the result would be the same—Zach would probably top six feet. But *someday* wasn't any consolation for today.

He eyed the figure slouching before him and said instead, "Let me see your hands. You can't start until they're healed."

Zach thrust them toward him. The bandages were gone, and while the skin was reddened, the hands didn't appear to be painful.

Deke nodded, "Okay, you'll be wearing gloves, so they should be fine. The first thing is safety, and it's always first when you're working with power tools. So tie your shoelaces, tight, and get rid of the bling." Forestalling the frown he saw gathering, he added grimly, "Believe me, moving machine parts can snag and rip off an ear as quickly as a foot. And even if we can find it, the doc may or may not be able to re-attach it. We don't want to take the chance. Tomorrow, as soon as you're out of school, we'll get you a pair of work boots.

Zach gulped, chastened by the visual of bodily harm, "I have Doc Martens upstairs. Would they work?"

Two hundred dollar boots for a pubescent teen? Deke barely restrained a growl, what *was* his mother thinking? "If they are brand new, no. You're not ruining expensive footwear."

"They're broken in," Zach assured him, "I mowed lawns all summer last year to buy them on EBay." He frowned, "I've almost outgrown them; I'll need a new pair before long anyway."

Deke felt his molars unclamp, and he sighed, "They'll do fine. Go put them on and get back here pronto." His last words were addressed to the back of a rapidly disappearing figure.

In less than five minutes, Zach bounced out the back door, properly shod and carrying two fistfuls of chocolate chip cookies along with two water bottles clamped under his arm. He handed one cookie stack to Deke, and with the newly-emptied hand, turned over one of the bottles.

"Thanks," Deke unscrewed the bottle and took a long, cold drink. He perched on a sawhorse and poked a whole cookie in his mouth, groaning at the explosion of flavor.

"I know," Zach perched beside him. "Wednesdays are baking days at the day care. Always pays to come right home on Wednesdays." Deke hid a smile; so much for thinking his prompt appearance after school had anything to do with his eagerness to learn something about carpentry.

Slapping his palms against his jeans to remove the

last of the crumbs, he stood, “Okay, Zach, time to work.”

Zach followed eagerly. Deke could practically feel him vibrating from his excitement. He handed him one end of the fifty-foot tape measure. “I’ve finished framing in the room; now I’m ready to nail the sheeting on the exterior. He pointed to the sheets of plywood. We’re going to nail those to the outside now.” Together they picked up a board, laid it against the house, and while Zach held it, Deke nailed it in place.

Deke could see him eyeing the power gun and understood the fascination with it. On the next sheet, he leaned against the wall, holding it in place, and said, “Okay, Zach, pick up the nail gun, hold the head flush against the board, and press the trigger gently.”

He watched Zach gingerly pick up the tool and warned, “Be careful, nailing a body part, like your foot, to the floor is a really painful way to learn to be careful around power tools.”

“Have you ever done that?” Zach was intrigued.

“I accidentally nailed my shoe, which by the grace of God went in at an angle and missed my foot.”

“Lucky shot,” Zach breathed.

“Yes, if it had gotten my foot, I would have had to take the board to the hospital to get my foot free. These nails do not pull out easily.” He was glad to see a shudder go through Zach frame. Reality was a good thing when it came to potentially dangerous situations.

Watching how carefully Zach followed his instructions brought a lump to his throat. Thirteen was the age his kid would be today. The long-buried regret bubbled up, and he was surprised again at how fresh the pain was. He hadn’t thought about him—or her—for several years, well until the last few months at least.

Watching Zach as he awkwardly hammered nails, swung boards dangerously, and just generally got in the way more than he helped, Deke's heart ached with the knowledge that the son he once had as a promise would never work with him. He would never teach him how to use his hands or talk to him about whatever was interesting him at the moment. Never watch him play in a football game or act in a school play. And the pain of the loss grabbed him in a way he had never experienced before. Until now, what he had lost had been distant knowledge, but watching Zach, knowing that his son would have been the same age, and seeing in flesh, what he had lost in potential, brought new pain to him. Anyone who wouldn't protect his child didn't deserve another chance.

By the time it was too dark to work anymore, they had the sheeting attached, and Zach was huffing loudly from the unaccustomed exertion.

"Great," Deke said with satisfaction, looking at what they had accomplished. "First thing tomorrow I can begin working on the roof."

Zach sighed, "Sure wish I could stay home from school tomorrow and help, but Mom would probably say no."

"So would I," Deke assured him, "but never fear Skate Boy, you'll get all the carpentering you want in the next few weeks."

"Cool."

###

It had been a normal day, Chloe reflected as she rinsed off the counters. Nice to have one of those again. It was also nice to look out the window after school and see Zach instead of wondering where he was, who he was with, and what he was doing. She hoped he wasn't giving Deke any sass. She paused at the kitchen door, the upper pane showing Deke stowing his gear and Zach, apparently, helping willingly. He turned toward the house as Deke got into his truck, and she backed away, anxious not to be caught spying on her son. She was once again standing at the sink when he entered.

She turned to greet him and saw him fully in the overhead light. "Oh, no. Huh-uh." She advanced on him shaking her finger, "Take off those filthy clothes right now. You are not tracking that mud through my day care."

"What?" he looked down at himself. In Seattle any dirt quickly became a quagmire, and from all appearance, most of in the mud from her backyard clung to her son. He grinned at his appearance, "Okay. I'll chuck everything right here and head to the shower if you'll just leave."

"Going!" She suited action to her words and headed upstairs taking care not to look back and embarrass her son.

A few minutes later she heard his steps on the staircase, the bathroom door shut, and the sound of water as the shower turned on. She checked on the meatloaf she'd slipped into the oven during afternoon break, and then went back down to the laundry room off of the kitchen. She shook mud off his jeans and shirt into the backyard then stuffed the clothes into the washing machine, dumped in extra soap, and turned the setting on hot and heavy-duty. She figured she'd have to wash them at least twice to get them clean and hoped the plumbing could handle the dirt coming its way.

She picked up the boots to set aside for Zach to clean after supper. Her brows rose when she recognized his beloved Doc Martens. What on earth had Zach been thinking to wear them on a job site? Oh! Comprehension hit her. The heavy leather made them the closest thing to construction work boots Zach had. She hoped they lived up to their high price and survived this job, because Zach had saved all summer to purchase them, even second-hand.

She returned upstairs and finished preparing supper, finishing at the same time that Zach emerged from his shower in clean clothes.

"I'm starved," he announced pulling out his chair. He grabbed his glass of milk and emptied half of it before Chloe sat down. She thought about chiding his manners and the fact that they hadn't said grace but couldn't bear to break their fragile truce.

"You want to say grace?" She shook out her napkin and placed it in her lap.

"Sure," they bowed their heads. "Thanks, God, for the great meal Mom cooked and for me getting to help Deke today. Amen."

They settled in to dinner, and Chloe was surprised when Zach brought up the subject of the fire and his friends reaction, "They were all over me at school today, wanting to know why I hadn't run like they had," his voice was scornful. "I told them burning down someone's property was a stupid thing to do." Some of them thought I'd ratted on them to the cops.

She eyed him, trying to gauge his reaction to their accusations, "Why would they think that?" she carefully set her cup down, her heart pounding, "have the police been talking to them?"

"No, they just know that Deke caught me, and so they assumed that I squealed."

"What did you tell them?"

"That I hadn't told Deke any of their names, nor did I go to the police."

"Did they believe you?"

He shrugged, "I don't know. They shoved me once or twice, but then they left, so maybe. Anyway, Andrew was sitting with me, and he told them to lay off.

"Are all the kids at the skate park students at Fowler?

"No, a lot of them are dropouts, and most of the others go to the public school. A few of them, like TJ, go to Fowler. He's the richest kid in school. His dad's a neurosurgeon, and his mom is a state senator. He's an only kid, and his parents are gone a lot. He says they're going to build him his own skateboard park on their property." He lifted a shoulder in mild disbelief, "But he also said they were flying to St. Moritz for Christmas but now says that something came up and plans have changed."

He continued to shovel in the food, apparently unaware of how much new information he was revealing to her, "He is actually kind of geeky, like most of us at Fowler, but he seems to want to make all of us jealous. Like any of us care if his parents are rich," Zach's derision was clear. The skating code was plain: It's not who you are, it's what you can do on a board.

Zach continued in full space, saying, "Great, meatloaf. Andrew had a meatloaf sandwich in his lunch today. I didn't know anyone else liked them but me."

Oblivious to her shock that he had volunteered something about a friend, she struggled to keep the conversation going, "Maybe, Andrew's mom makes great meatloaf, just like yours does, and taught him how great it is with mustard and onion."

He examined the idea, "Maybe," he said doubtfully, "but Angela and Andrew's parents are lawyers. It doesn't seem like something lawyers would eat, does it?"

"I imagine lawyers eat regular American food just like everybody else. Is a meatloaf sandwich really that unusual? What do your other friends bring for lunch?"

"Well, the guys usually just buy chips or maybe eat a hot lunch, and the girls are usually sucking down yogurt because they're afraid of getting fat." His voice was full of disdain about the females of the species.

She felt fear and pain mingle within her. There was just too much happening in his life of which she was not a part, and while she was thankful he was being open, it was painful reflecting how off-track their relationship had become. He was barely a teenager; surely they shouldn't be on separate roads, yet. She swallowed the food in her mouth and took the plunge, "Zach, I can't live like this."

His head shot up, and he gazed at her with wide eyes.

"Normally, we haven't been talking. I don't know any of the kids you hang out with." She inhaled deeply, "I know you're angry at life right now. And because I have instigated a lot of the changes you are having to deal with, you are angry at me too."

Zach mumbled something. She overrode, "Yes, Zach, you are angry at me. I know it. And you know what? I can handle you being angry at me, but what I cannot handle is you shutting me out of your life like you're simply going to pretend I don't exist anymore."

"I don't do that," he mumbled.

"Yes, Zach, you do. You are angry, you don't like your life, you hate Seattle, you miss your Dad, and you wish you were anywhere except living here with me. But know something, Buster? We're stuck with each other for at least another five years. So we'd better learn to deal."

She sat waiting for his response. When nothing came she decided to lay it all out on the table, "Zach, why don't you bring any friends home? You had a lot of them who came over in California, and here I don't know anybody you hang out with. Is it because you don't want them to know you live above a day care?"

Zach was silent then he lifted his shoulder but didn't look up to meet her eyes, "I dunno. I guess home just doesn't feel like home anymore without dad." She felt the pain as if it was almost physical at what her son had lost, "And most of the kids I hang out with don't live this direction but over by Fremont." He finally looked up, "It doesn't have anything to do with living above The Perfect Child, Mom. I just haven't found anyone I like well enough to know beyond skating yet. When I find another person who likes to play war games as much as I do, then maybe I'll invite someone over."

"Okay," she tried to smile normally, "but you're always welcome to bring friends home anytime. Don't forget that."

###

On Thursday, Deke worked hard all day. Rain had fallen during the night, but the day had been clear, and like everyone in the northwest, when it stopped raining you wanted to get outside as much as possible. He hadn't noticed the afternoon waning; he hadn't even been aware that it was time for Zach to show up, until he came zooming around the corner of the house, fleeing as if the police were hot on his tail. Catching sight of Deke, he jerked to a stop, and then nonchalantly walked toward the house.

Deke eyed him, "Something the matter?" he asked casually. He knew something had happened, but he wasn't sure if Zach would tell him.

"Nope, nothing. Be out in a minute," the teen said airily, leaping up into the sunroom and heading into the kitchen without a backward glance.

Deke studied the closed door for a moment, then laid down his board and walked to the edge of the house to gaze down the driveway.

At the bottom of the driveway, a group of four teens milled around, smoking cigarettes, and talking amongst themselves. One of them spotted Deke and nudged the others, jerking his head up the driveway. They all silently stared at each other, and then at the unspoken command of the leader, spun around and headed down the block.

What was that about? He watched them until they disappeared from sight then turned toward the house. Zach's face hovered in the day care kitchen window for a moment then he pulled back and disappeared. When he exited five minutes later, neither of them referred to the incident.

Chapter 10

The following week was normal and placid, and Chloe hugged to herself the pleasure of not having conflict. She continued to inspect what had been accomplished, just before Zach was expected home. Not sure how it began, she also carried a hot mug of coffee for Deke. She told herself it was because it would taste better than a cup out of his thermos lid.

She tried to express her thanks to him for giving Zach something worthwhile to do, "He's really enjoying working with his hands."

"Yeah?" He grinned, and by the tilt of his smile, she knew he was about to tease her, "His work wardrobe leaves something to be desired. Doc Marten's are not work boots, and I almost had a heart attack thinking you had bought something that expensive for a thirteen year old."

"Well, then you must have been glad to learn that he earned them himself," she retorted smugly.

Later that afternoon, watching Zach measure and cut a board, Deke admitted to himself that he enjoyed Zach's company. He had been put off by the clothing and attitude, but after spending time with him, he was beginning to believe that Zach was just exhibiting normal teen angst, not true, dangerous rebellion. With a project to become involved in, he was a fun kid to talk to, and he obviously had a manual dexterity gene in his makeup because he caught on quickly. Deke found he didn't have to explain anything more than once and that each day saw

Zach demonstrating more dexterity in building.

"What kind of a guy was your dad?" he inquired casually. He had a feeling that Zach needed to talk about him, if for no other reason than to keep him alive in his mind.

"He was the best. I really miss him though. I always thought Mom was the tough parent, but while he was alive, I would never have been allowed to have a Mohawk or grunge clothes."

"Wouldn't have happened, huh?"

"Are you kidding?" He narrowed his eyes and assessed this evidence of change, "I would never have even asked to do any of this when he was alive."

"So why did you ask after he died?"

A shrug, then, "I was just angry at everything and decided that I needed to become someone else, since I wasn't going to be the same Zach I'd been for twelve years." He looked at Deke over his shoulder, mischief in his eyes, "Imagine my surprise when Mom said yes, because then I had to do it."

Deke snorted, "That's a bummer, getting what you wished."

Zach opened his eyes wide, "Tell me about it. Not only that, when you dress a certain way, it defines the kids who are willing to be your friends. All of a sudden the edgy, marginal kids that I never knew thought I was cool, and the kids I would normally be friends with avoided me."

Deke laughter bellowed out at Zach's wry expression of being caught by his own shenanigans, "That's what you get when you set a trap, sometimes you catch yourself."

"The only bright side that I can see is that I'm almost fourteen and surely at fourteen I can claim maturity and decide I'm ready for a change. The piercings will grow over, and thankfully, the tattoos are henna so they will fade before Christmas."

Still chuckling, Deke asked casually, "I need to run to the hardware store down on Queen Anne, would you like to ride with me?" He nodded toward his old pickup, not sure if the teen would consider himself above riding in it.

"Yeah,"

"Wait," Deke cautioned, "you've got to ask your mom first. I can't just decide to take you somewhere without her knowing."

"Sure, I'll be right back." He flew into the house and back out in a matter of seconds, climbing into the cab and slamming the door, "Cool, four on the floor. These old trucks are sweet."

They didn't return for over an hour. By that time, Chloe had left Tasha in charge of closing up and gone upstairs to prepare dinner. Zach came barreling through the door of the apartment, followed more slowly by Deke.

Deke felt awkward standing in the doorway but he needed to discuss tomorrow's work with her so he'd followed Zach up. She turned from her son and smiled at him, silently acknowledging her gratitude for his kindness to him. Before he could speak, Zach swung back to his mom, "Can Deke stay for supper? What are we having?" He poked his nose over her shoulder, "Fried chicken! Deke, you like chicken don't you?"

Deke looked uncomfortable and for some reason that made Chloe feel protective, "If you like fried chicken, you are welcome to stay and eat with us," she smiled.

"If you're sure there's enough, and it's no bother."

"None at all," she said briskly, turning back to the skillet of sizzling meat. "Pull up a chair, I'm just about ready to make the gravy and then we'll eat. That is," she turned to Zach, "as soon as you set the table."

"No prob, Mom," he stuck his hands under the kitchen faucet, wet them, and dried them on a corner of her apron.

Deke's brows rose—an apron? He didn't know any woman still wore them. He thought she looked cute as a bug's ear in her kind of retro, June Cleaver outfit, but he didn't think he'd be telling her that any time soon.

In a matter of minutes they were all at the kitchen table, tucking into the delicious meal. "Something about food that someone else cooks," he said, buttering his third biscuit, "it always tastes fantastic."

Dinner was quiet, she knew that Maleficent sat beneath the table and begged scraps from Zach, but she wasn't aware that Deke also joined him in sneaking tidbits, until Maleficent hacked up a bite of broccoli. Zach wouldn't eat broccoli, wouldn't even have it on his plate, so it had to have come from Deke's plate.

She leveled a stare at each of them, "Do not feed that cat people food."

Zach grinned, "Mom, she's the only cat in the universe that will eat vegetables. That makes her unique, one of a kind."

She eyed Deke's arm that was out of sight below the table and said, "Deke Hudson, you'll be cleaning up the mess if you don't stop it."

"Yes, ma'am," he grinned at Zach.

"Mom," Zach turned to her, "now that I'm almost off all grounding, a bunch of us want to go to the arcade by Fowler tomorrow after school. Could I go with them?"

Chloe pondered the request, "Have you asked your boss if you can take a day off."

Deke was silently amused; he had bet himself that she would cave. He especially liked Zach's assessment of being *almost* off grounding.

Zach turned to Deke, "May I skip one day? Please?"

Deke took a gulp of his coffee, "It's okay with me, if your mom agrees. You've been real good help."

Chloe smiled at Zach's flush of pride and responded, "Who are you going with? I don't want you hanging around with anyone from the skate park."

"Actually, it's Andrew and Angela, plus two other kids from the youth group. They go to public school, but we're planning to meet them there." He looked to Deke, "It's Jared Toomby and Ben Hembrick."

Chloe eyes switched to Deke, and he nodded, smiling slightly, "I know their families. Good kids, both of them, if that is any reassurance to you."

"Okay, then. What time will you be home?

"Oh, I'll be home by supper," he assured her, "but I'd need some money, fifty bucks should do it."

Deke, in the process of taking another swallow, snorted while Chloe stared at her son in amazement, "Fifty bucks? Are you crazy? Who are you hanging out with, Zach? Tell me no parent is handing their thirteen-year-old fifty dollars to play an afternoon of games."

Zach didn't even blink, "Didn't think you'd give it to me. Just thought I might catch you in a good mood."

"If you want me in a good mood, I'd suggest that you remember that I cooked supper, so it's your turn to do the dishes."

"Mom, I have a paper due tomorrow, would you do them for me please?" Deke watched Zach watch the emotions flit over his mom's face and knew, just as Zach did, the exact moment she gave in again.

"Well, okay, but just this one time."

Zach hugged her, "Thanks, Mom, you're the best." He left the room at a lope, and the slam of his bedroom door followed soon after.

Deke leaned over, thunking his head on the table top, "You are ruining that kid."

She ruffled up like a wet hen, "Families help each other," she informed him haughtily.

"Teenagers play anyone who will let them," he returned.

She eyed him in irritation, "Why do I think that a hired hand doesn't need to have an opinion about my parenting skills or lack thereof?"

He grinned, knowing her annoyance came because she knew he was right, "Zach's potentially a good kid, but you're allowing him to set the rules. I know it's been rough for both of you in the last couple of years, but don't undo all the good work you've put into his life."

She sighed and looked over his shoulder for a long moment then spoke in a quiet voice of desperation, "I'm afraid I'm losing my son. He barely talks to me; he resents me. Anything I can do to keep him liking me is worth it."

He responded bluntly, "No it's not."

"Oh?" Her delicate eyebrows rose in an arch,

"Have you ever raised a teenager?"

"No, I was just one once, and I know a line when I hear it. You've got it backwards; you're going to lose him if you *don't* take back control." He broke into another grin at the mutiny in her face. Her hair fairly glowed with temper.

He leaned forward and captured her hand in his, "He doesn't need expensive clothes or high-priced entertainment handed to him. He needs to learn to be happy with what he can provide or make himself. It doesn't take fifty dollars to go to the arcade with his friends. Shoot, I could take all three of us on a day-long date for seventy-five bucks. How on earth could he spend fifty?"

"Well, I didn't give him fifty dollars, now did I? I happen to agree he doesn't need that much either." She was diverted, "However, I don't think you have taken anyone on a date in quite a few years if you think you could entertain three of us – nicely – for only seventy-five dollars. What century are you living in?"

All four legs of the chair hit the floor, and he extended a hand to her across the table, "I can take all three of us out for a great day on Saturday and spend less than seventy-five dollars to do it. Bet me?"

She eyed him warily. She really didn't think it was wise to go anywhere with him, Deke was too unsettling to be around. However, it would be great to make him eat his words. She clasped his hand in hers and shook it firmly, "It's a deal."

"Don't you want to ask Zach if he wants to go? I'd hate for it to be just you and me," his eyes dared her.

She felt her face flush, "He's grounded, remember? He'll go wherever I tell him to. What time should we be ready?"

"Eight o'clock," he stood and pushed in his chair tidily, "I'll pick you both up, and don't eat breakfast. I'll bring it."

###

She couldn't sleep. She realized Deke's words tonight had shaken her. It was time she admitted that Zach was teetering on the brink of delinquency, and she needed help. She closed her eyes and prayed, "God, I have asked you so many times in the past months what Zach needed. But I realize that in my usual manner, I haven't stopped to listen. Please show me what it is I need to be doing."

Each of them had handled their grief differently: she had dulled the pain by crowding more and more into her life. Only, she was insane to think that moving to a new city and a new house and beginning a new business would leave enough time to add volunteering. While Zach, losing home and friends and adjusting to a new home and school environment, had seen his skateboard as the only constant in his life. He'd enjoyed skateboarding in California, but it had only been one part of his life. Here it had become everything to him, and he had pursued it and been willing to change in order to fit in. Instead of seeing beneath the surface of his demands to fit in with his new buddies, she had caved and allowed him license in areas she knew, and had known then, were dangerous to him.

She sat up, turned on the light, and picked up the pad and pen on her nightstand. She wrote: Cancel ALL Volunteering. As she turned out her light, feeling lighter than she had in weeks, she reminded herself that she was the only one with the epiphany and there were more rocky times ahead for her relationship with Zach as she resumed her responsibilities of a mother and guide to her son.

Immediately, like a refreshing breeze within her soul, she felt the Holy Spirit's presence, and His living words, *My grace is sufficient for you.* He was the God of new beginnings.

###

At home Deke unloaded his truck, putting everything he wouldn't need tomorrow tidily back in its designated spot. He opened the passenger door and Woofer bounded out like he was a pup again, happy to be outside. They walked the perimeter of the lot, something he had done every night since the fire. It was a beautiful evening, the setting sun leaving a rosy glow to the heavens. Woofer sniffed and nosed his way along, ecstatic at all the new scents to explore.

They finished on Mrs. Watanabe's back step, Woofer curling up in his accustomed spot. Deke knocked perfunctorily then stepped into the kitchen, calling out, "Mrs. Watanabe?"

"In here," she spoke from the living room. He walked into the room, pausing as he did each time, to admire her view from the front window. She took the glasses off her nose, folded them tidily, and gestured for him to sit down.

"You're late if you're just getting home from work," she commented.

"Yes, Chloe and Zach invited me to stay for supper."

She eyed him, "You like the widow and her son?"

"Yeah I do." More than he wanted to admit even to himself, "She keeps me on my toes, and he's becoming less a pain in the neck every day. He's surprisingly good at carpentry, seems to have a real knack for it."

"Do you and Ms. Uptight have anything in

common?" She was genuinely curious. Despite living most of her life in the States, her culture was deeply steeped within her. Even Ichito, her son and Deke's friend, though born in the United States, had only considered taking a bride from within the Japanese community.

"Well," he paused to allow himself to consider Chloe and himself as a couple, analyzing the concept in his mind to see what it would look like, "we have the same faith."

She nodded. She knew how important the Lord God was to him and would never expect him to consider a companion who didn't hold the same beliefs.

"Sounds like she could be the one, but would you be able to be a stepfather to a teenager?"

He almost smiled. Whenever he had allowed himself to daydream about becoming a father, the child he envisioned certainly hadn't been a smart-mouthed thirteen-year-old. He wondered if other parents wondered how they'd started out with a sweet tiny baby and ended up with a tattooed, pierced teen.

"No," he said gruffly, "I don't think that would work."

She eyed him thoughtfully for a long moment, but didn't make any comment. She knew there was something from his past that haunted him, but she did not pry.

He stayed for only a few minutes, making sure there wasn't anything that she needed and headed home. He fed Woofer a scoop of dog chow, listened to the messages on his machine, and went to bed.

Lying in bed two hours later, he realized it was going to be one of those sleepless nights again. He contemplated simply lying there and resting but knew from experience that old images would begin to replay in his mind and he wouldn't get any rest.

Finally at one a.m., he threw on some old clothes and, leaving Woofer snoozing in his bed, went out his back door. He stood on the steps and contemplated the night sky, breathing in the quiet then he walked across the parking area and unlocked his shop. Clicking on the lights, he inhaled the scent of sawdust and wood oil. He picked up a dresser drawer he was dove-tailing and concentrated on getting the fit tight. The soothing rhythm of working with the wood relaxed him, allowing him to forget everything except what his hands were doing.

Two hours later he set aside the finished drawer, cleaned up, exited the building, locking it behind him, and re-entered the house. This time he slept until his alarm sounded at six a.m.

Chapter 11

Deke was lounging against the side of his pickup Saturday morning, dressed in jeans, work boots, and a flannel shirt over a white t-shirt, when Chloe stumbled out the front door. Zach was already depositing his skateboard into the bed of the truck.

Deke straightened and smiled, and suddenly, Chloe didn't feel quite so grumpy, "Good morning," he handed her a steaming cup of Seattle's Best. Putting his hand in his pocket, he pulled a selection of creams and sugars, "Didn't know if you needed any of these," she shook her head inhaling the heavenly scent.

Finally, her vocal chords were oiled enough to speak, "Good morning, it's a beautiful day. You lucked out."

He looked smug, "Not luck. Planning."

"Sure, weather forecasters get paid big bucks to be wrong about the weather, but you can plan good weather just like that."

He didn't reply – he was getting good at ignoring her, "Get in," he opened his door and motioned for her to slide in. She scooted to the middle, Zach slid in from the passenger side, and she was suddenly bookended by the males. Before he started the truck, Deke reached into his pocket and handed her a scrap of paper, "Okay, I have seventy-five dollars cash for today, and here is our first receipt; you get to be the bookkeeper." She glanced down and saw that the total for two coffees and one hot chocolate was $5.42.

He pointed with smug pride, “Notice, I chose McDonald’s and not Starbucks.” He slanted a glance at her, his eyes brimming with mischief, “If you’d been just a tad older, I could have gotten a senior discount, and the drinks would have been cheaper.”

“Thanks,” she said, tucking the receipt into the pocket of her flannel shirt and managing to dig an elbow into his ribs while doing so. Deke winced and shifted as he expertly backed out of the driveway and wheeled down the street.

“Where we going?” Zach had never sounded so enthusiastic at eight a.m.

“We’re going to breakfast,” Deke headed down the Alaskan Viaduct and, in just a few minutes, pulled into Waterfront Park at the wharf. He opened his door and hopped out. Chloe and Zach stared at each other for a moment, then Zach shrugged, pushed open his door, and Chloe followed.

Deke lifted a small cooler from his pickup and a blanket, “Come on, let’s sit on the grass and watch the ferries while we eat.” He led the way to a vantage point and spread out the cover. All three sat, and Deke lifted the lid of the cooler. Fragrant aromas drifted into the air. He reached in and passed around foil-wrapped bundles, “Homemade breakfast sandwiches.” He reached in again and pulled up a bag of freshly-washed grapes. The sandwiches were delicious – the scrambled egg fluffy and the bacon crisp. When partnered with the coffee it was delicious.

“This is fantastic,” Chloe took a second bite.

“Cool,” Zach enthused. Deke noticed he’d inhaled his sandwich in four bites and reached back into the cooler and handed Zach a second bundle. Zach dug into it like a starving hound.

Chloe sipped her coffee and felt the tight muscles in her shoulders begin relax. She looked across Elliott Bay and spotted a ferry leaving the terminal, probably heading toward Vashon Island. She sighed; it had been so long since she'd ridden the ferries. They finished the meal, watching the morning brighten, and the wharf begin to wake up. Below them, people began to fill the sidewalks as shopkeepers opened their doors and extended their awnings. Ferries docked at the terminal, unloaded and reloaded, and pulled back out again. After a while Deke gathered the remains of their meal and dumped them in the cooler, closing the lid.

"What now?" Zach seemed up for whatever came next.

"We're going to fly kites," Deke said standing and extending a hand to Chloe. She grabbed it and allowed herself to be pulled up, then stooped to shake out the blanket and fold it neatly.

He drove down the wharf to the Water Taxi stand at Pier 55, paid the fare for three, and they climbed in for the twelve-minute ride across the bay. At Sea Crest Park, they had to grab the shuttle which deposited them at Alki Beach minutes later. At the beach, he reached inside his daypack and pulled out three kites.

"Cool," Zach exclaimed grabbing Sponge Bob SquarePants. Chloe looked at him in disbelief; the kite must have cost all of $2.50 at K-Mart. It was not cool; it was the simplest kite, one used by preschoolers, and he acted like it was priceless. Deke handed him a spool of string, then reached inside and handed Chloe a kite (and the receipt). She unwrapped hers—it was Cruella DaVille. She eyed Deke, and he returned her look with an innocent

"*Whaaaat?*" as he unrolled and snapped together his Bob the Builder kite.

In just a few minutes, all three of them were running down the beach, launching their kites and seeing whose would fly the highest. The sun blazed warm on their backs; the quiet on the water was broken by the snap and rustle of their kites, as they swooped and dived, trailing along behind them.

The two-and-a-half mile long pedestrian walkway was populated by beach volleyball players, sun worshipers, and beachcombers in the summer; however, it was virtually deserted today. She knew that most of the beaches on Elliott Bay were covered in rock and shells, and was excited to see that on Alki there was actual sand. It appeared to be a great place to get some exercise and take in a great view of the Seattle skyline.

They spent several hours launching their kites, laughing at the predicaments the others got into, and dodging each others' strings so they wouldn't tangle. Chloe could feel herself decompressing, her spirits lifting, all while the sunshine and laughter soothed her soul.

Chloe tired first. She dug out a depression in the sand and curled up to the watch the guys. After a while, Deke rolled in his kite and plopped down next to Chloe. They were quiet, watching Zach still running up and down the beach, yelling at the seagulls and flying his kite. They sat enjoying the warmth, the sound the water, and the wind on their backs.

She noticed his eyes following her son, happily clomping up and down the beach, and it reminded her of something she'd wanted to ask him for a while, "May I ask you a personal question?"

He didn't move for a moment then lifted his head and stared at her, "I guess so."

"What is it about my son that bothers you?" She waved off the start of his reply, "That's probably the wrong word to use. You are great with him—he thinks you walk on water—but I see you staring at him sometimes. Not in the usual *teens are such a mess* reaction that can be normal, but as if he's a puzzle you're trying to solve."

He looked fully into her eyes, his incredulous. "Yes, yes," he breathed, "that's exactly the way he makes me feel." He rubbed the back of his neck and took a deep breath, "I look at him that way because he shows me what I've missed from my life all these years." He hunched forward, clasped his hands, and gave a deep sigh, "When I was seventeen my girlfriend and I got too friendly, and she got pregnant." He stopped, and she had the feeling he was afraid to continue. She just waited, a profound sadness filling her at his pain. "She didn't want to be pregnant, her parents did not want her to be pregnant, and I certainly didn't want to be a father … so we took the easy way out. She had an abortion."

Involuntarily her hand strayed and rested on his knotted fists, "I am so sorry, Deke. You just didn't know the ramifications of such an action."

He took a breath, "So I look at Zach, and I wander what kind of a father I would have been if we had made another choice. And, I guess, I feel sadness that I will never be a dad."

She was confused, "Why would that preclude you ever being a father?"

He stared at her, his eyes hard, "Didn't you hear me? I killed my child."

Her heart broke at the misery and pain in his eyes. She was silent, hesitant to speak. Afraid that anything she said would hurt him more, "Deke, everyone acts upon what they know at the time. We make choices according to the information we have. You were not born again when you were seventeen. You did not understand that this was a living child. You believed the information you were fed from others who say that an embryo is simply a mass of cells. The important thing for you to grasp is that forgiveness means it's all been washed away. God doesn't hold you hostage to this sin; you are holding this sin against yourself. You will make a fantastic father; you need to let go of your past and allow yourself to look into your future. You need a baby, Hudson," she grinned at him.

"How do you know so much?" He turned his head to gaze at her somberly.

She smiled gently, "No, no, I have never aborted a child, but I've had friends who did. I watched helplessly as they spiraled into drugs or depression or promiscuous behavior, and I decided to find out everything I could to help them. I began volunteering at a crisis pregnancy center near my college and discovered that no matter how much you rationalize your actions, your spirit knows that what you did was wrong. I took training and began to help the women who ran the recovery groups. Since I had never—Thank you, Jesus—experienced their pain, I can't lead a workshop, but I can help out with organizing them and, most of all, pray for the participants' recovery."

She shifted and looked at him, "We are discovering that not only mothers experience this pain, but fathers, also. So now there are recovery groups for fathers of aborted children, to help them heal. You need to attend a class, Deke. You need to deal with this mountain in your life and move on to a guilt-free life. You are suffering from Post Abortion Trauma."

He snorted, looking over her shoulder into the distance. "Yeah, yeah, psycho-babble is just what I need."

"Post Abortion Trauma is likened to Post Traumatic Stress Disorder. I certainly can't remember all the symptoms but how about these: guilt, trouble sleeping, eating disorders, drug abuse, detachment..."

Something she had said grabbed him, she could tell, "Do you experience any of these symptoms on an on-going basis?"

He shrugged, "Well, maybe, but it's been fourteen years since I was seventeen. The fact that these feelings show up now means that the abortion isn't what's causing them, doesn't it?"

"No, it means that only now is your body processing what happened and probably that you are now ready to deal with the effects of it on yourself."

She reached across and laid her hand on top of his fist. "Men are welcome to PAS classes."

"I don't know, Chloe. Spilling my guts to strangers isn't really my thing."

"Not even if it would garner you the ability to forgive yourself? An easy conscience is a priceless thing."

The moment passed as Zach, finally admitting he was tired, pulled in his kite and plopped beside his mom. "This is fun," he panted happily. "Do you do stuff like this a lot, Deke?"

"Just pack up and go for the day? Yeah, I do. Only usually I go on my hog."

"You have a Harley?" Zach's delight could hardly be contained. Chloe's head whipped around, and she speared Deke with a death glare that said, "Don't even think about it."

He held her eyes for moment, before he answered, "Yeah, I have a Harley Hog. I got it the day I left the

Army and went all over the United States and Canada on it, even down a little ways into Mexico. It was a cheap way to see the country and decompress. I just strapped on my bedroll and took off for six months getting the kinks out of my spirit after Afghanistan."

It didn't seem possible, but Zach's worship shifted up another notch, "You were in Afghanistan? That is really cool."

"That was anything but cool." Deke's low voice was final, "I had nightmares for months."

"Oh." Zach was momentarily wordless as he processed Deke's comment. He waited, hoping that Deke would enlarge on it, but when it was apparent the subject was closed he asked, "What are we going to do now? I'm hungry."

Deke and Chloe both laughed.

"Of course you are," she said.

Deke bought Zach and himself hotdogs with sauerkraut at a vendor, but Chloe declined. He handed her the receipt as they walked back to the ferry terminal, and Deke revealed the next stop, "The Aquarium. It's kids' free day. Last one to the dock is a loser," and he sprinted off. Zach tore after him laughing and yelling like a banshee.

Chloe didn't attempt to keep up with them but strolled along, enjoying the fresh air and the sounds of their laughter as it blew back to her on the breeze. When she joined them a few minutes later, they were sitting at a picnic table arm wrestling. Even with a handicap Deke easily won. Laughing, Zach challenged, "I demand a rematch in a month."

Deke nodded, "And you just might win. Manual labor is a great way to build muscle, and I can already see you're developing in your arms."

As Chloe watched her son's chest puff out at the complement, she fought off tears. Deke's kindness and understanding of a young male's ego filled her with unexplained emotions.

They spent an hour-and-a-half wandering around the aquarium, staying quite a while at the otter exhibit, laughing at their antics. They were early enough in the day that the crowd was minimal, but by the time they exited a little after one o'clock, there was a long line of impatient families waiting to get in.

"Okay," Zach shrugged his jacket back on; he'd removed it in the aquarium and tried to hand it to Chloe to hold, but Deke had scowled at him, and grinning, Zach had tied it around his waist.

Deke announced their next destination, "We're going shopping at Pike Place Market." They climbed up the hill to 1st and Pine and the year-round open market.

At the entrance to the market he stopped and pulled three five-dollar bills out of his pocket, "Okay, we've each got half an hour to find the tackiest thing we can purchase with five dollars. The winner gets to pick where we'll eat lunch." He handed a bill to each of them, and Zach tore off immediately.

He grinned at Chloe, "Better get going; I come here two or three times a week. I know all the trinkets the market sells."

She stared at it as if it were a snake. He suppressed a grin; he would bet she had never done anything just to be silly in her life, but she surprised him. After a moment she swiped her bill from his hand, gave him a *You-wanna-bet* stare, and headed out. Twenty minutes later, she marched back up and joined the males who were already waiting.

"Okay, Mom, ladies first; show us what you got." Zach was fairly dancing with excitement.

"Ta-da!" She withdrew her purchase from the bag with a flourish. It was a bobblehead Chihuahua, which she presented to Deke, "For your truck window." He bellowed with laughter.

"Oh, mine is better," Zach boasted. He displayed his choice, which he was wearing—a glow-in-the-dark ,skull-and-crossbones wrap bracelet. Chloe shook her head in despair.

They both turned expectantly to see what Deke had found, and he opened his hand to reveal a tiny crystal space needle.

"You cheated," Zach accused, while Chloe smiled and cupped the tiny image in the palm of her hand. "It's beautiful," she whispered, and Zach's accusation trailed off as he looked between his mother and Deke in suspicion.

Deke smiled, "I know, I cheated, and therefore I lost. But I thought it was a nice memento of today for you."

He looked at Zach, "So, Zach, who do you think won, you or your mom?"

Zach groaned, "Mom. There's nothing tackier than that stupid Chihuahua in a window."

Chloe smiled in satisfaction, and Deke turned to her, "Okay, Mom, where do you want to eat lunch?"

In a matter of minutes, they were at Pier 54 and Ivars Fish House, waiting outside on the deck for their orders of fish and chips to materialize. Overhead the seagulls kept up a cacophony of cries, well aware that there was plenty of plunder for their begging. Seattle natives might ignore them, but there were always plenty of tourists who would give in to their shameless cries and toss them scraps. Next door a local fishing boat pulled up and bartered with passing tourists for its catch. The sun shone its bright light, and the wind tossed up mini-whitecaps. Chloe was aware of the perfection of the moment and savored it, because it had been a long time since she'd felt so at peace.

###

After they had eaten their fill, they wandered along the waterfront, watching the crowds and the water traffic. On the way to lunch they had stopped by the truck for Zach to grab his skateboard, and he cruised on it beside Chloe and Deke. She was filled with contentment, the sun was warm on her shoulders, and she felt more relaxed than she could remember being in many months. As they wound in and out of tourists, Deke took her hand to keep her by his side and retained it after there was no longer a need to do so. She was aware that it felt comfortable and right to hold his hand.

After a while, the breeze freshened and Chloe gave a small shiver, and by mutual consent they turned back toward the truck. Once the skateboard was stowed in the back and they were all in the cab, she expected Deke to head back to their house, assuming the day was over. She was aware that she was sad to see it end.

Stretching back against the seat, Deke dug into his pocket and withdrew assorted bills and coins which he handed to Zach, "Okay, you count it and see how much of the seventy-five bucks is left."

Chloe, afraid of her secret delight that the day wasn't ending after all, felt she ought to offer him a way out and murmured, "We could just go home, I'm sure you have a lot that needs to be done."

Deke stared at her, "The day's not over until the seventy-five bucks is gone, lady." He turned to Zach, "How much?"

"Nineteen dollars and seven cents."

Deke nodded, "Sounds like just enough for a pizza wouldn't you say?" He started the truck, pulled out, and headed up the street.

As she got ready for bed that night she couldn't help smiling at the memory of the day. It really had been wonderful. They had picked up two pizzas at Papa Murphy's and taken them back to the apartment to bake. She had added a salad—much to Zach's dismay—and they had sat together on the couch, the coffee table pulled close for a table, to eat and watch Star Wars. Afterwards she had popped popcorn to fill up the empty spaces that Zach and Deke were positive were still there.

As Deke prepared to leave, he turned to Zach, extended his hand and perplexed, Zach reached out to meet his. Deke shook his hand firmly, "Zach, consider your debt paid. I wasn't interested in the money so much as your willingness to accept responsibility. You did so like a man, and I am proud of you."

Zach's face was strangely vulnerable as he looked into Deke's and he swallowed before responding, "Thanks. But I will still be glad to help you after school if you want."

Deke smiled, "Be glad to have you anytime, Zach. You're a good helper."

As she walked Deke to the door he said, "Hold out your hand." Perplexed, she extended her hand, and he dropped a collection of coins into her palm and closed her fingers around them. "That's the end of the bet. I think we got our money's worth today, don't you?"

She had smiled back, "Yes, and thank you, Deke, it was a great day."

He leaned in close, and she felt his cheek lay against the top of her head, as his arms came around her. She felt herself wanting to melt and stringently held herself erect, irritated at her traitorous self. He held her for a long moment, then lifted his head and looked in her eyes somberly, "I need to remember that I don't like bossy women and mouthy teens, or I'm going to be in over my head."

She stiffened in his embrace, "Well, don't let me keep you," she snapped. Deke simply chuckled as if she had confirmed his warning, gave her one last hug, and went out to his truck.

Chapter 12

Sunday was a lazy day. After talking it over with Zach, they had tried All Saints, and he seemed to enjoy going there. She no longer had to argue with him to attend the youth services. She already felt a kinship with the members and had been invited to join a women's Bible study. Andrew and Angela's parents had introduced themselves the first week, and Deke had made a point of introducing her to the parents who were currently leading youth Bible studies.

After the morning service, she and Zach went out to lunch. He was excited because today was the first day he was off grounding, so as soon as they got home, he grabbed his board and headed out the door.

She didn't think anything about it until she noticed it was almost six, and she hadn't heard him return. She went out on the front porch and looked up and down the street. Their block, unlike most of those in Queen Anne, was fairly level, with a gentle downward slant, which in Zach's opinion made it a perfect place to try new maneuvers. So it was not uncommon for him to spend hours skateboarding right out front. But he wasn't anywhere within sight. She punched in number 2 on her speed dial, only to hear his cell phone ringing from his bedroom. Great, he'd gone out without his phone.

Finally, at six-thirty she gave in her to fears and got into her Volvo to drive by all the places she knew he frequented. She didn't see Zach or any other kids out plying their boards. By seven she admitted she was very scared. She didn't know who to call or where to turn to help, but suddenly, remembering Deke's kindness to Zach, she dialed the number on the Home Construction business card he'd given her. She didn't figure he would be in the office, but she hoped that there were be an emergency contact number on the voice mail.

"Hello?" His deep voice answered almost immediately.

All her carefully prepared talk disappeared in an instant, "Deke, Zach hasn't come home. He's been gone all day, and I can't find him at any of his usual places." She stopped. What did she think he could do that she couldn't? She realized that she was tired of raising a teen all on her own, and she longed for someone to share her fears with.

Deke's voice broke in, "I don't think he's out back, but I'll check and call you right back."

She stood holding the receiver and staring into space. Where could he be?

Meanwhile, Deke, snagged a jacket off the hook by his back door and grabbed a flashlight. Woofer, happy at the prospect of a walk leaped out the door ahead of him. Deke called him to heel and headed to the back of his property. Behind his storage shed, most of the land remained undisturbed, and he could have walked it blindfolded. Woofer explored all the fun new smells since he'd been out a few hours ago.

"Zach?" He called out as he approached. It was completely dark by now and as he figured, nobody appeared to be around. Suddenly Woofer's ears pricked, "What do you see boy?" Woofer whined and wiggled anxiously. "Go on, show me what you hear." The dog bounded into the tall weeds and Deke followed. By doubling his body in half, he pushed his way through the natural barrier into a small clearing. Zach sat there all alone in the dark. That he had been crying was evident by his jump and quick swipe at his face when Deke's flashlight hit him. Deke immediately redirected the beam.

"Your mom's getting worried, Zach. Are you okay?

"I'm fine," his usual sharp, unconcerned tone was missing. His defenses were down.

"Anything I can do to help?" Deke casually dropped beside him and pulled Woofer into a one-armed hug. "Your mom's going out of her mind worrying about you."

"I'm sorry," Zach reached out to rub Woofer's head. He concentrated on rubbing Woofer's hair just the right way and finally sighed, "It just all hit me. Yesterday we were like a family again, having a man around. I miss my dad, and this afternoon at the skate park, we were just talking, and the guys, all of them, were dissing their parents. Most of them only live with one parent, but even those who have both of them don't like their dads or hate their dads or wish their dads were dead. And here I am wishing like anything that I could have my dad back…it just doesn't seem fair, you know?" His voice was low.

"Yeah, it must suck to have known a real dad and then have him gone."

Zach looked up in surprise, "Didn't you know your dad?"

"No, I never knew my dad or mom. I grew up in foster homes."

They both sat quietly for a few minutes. Then Deke offered, "But at least you know what a good dad is like, Zach. That's something I and, evidently your buddies, never have known. You're one of the lucky ones.

At least to me you are. Even if I couldn't have had a dad forever, just to have known one and known he loved me would have been the greatest thing, I think."

"Yeah, it just sucks, you know? Nothing's the same anymore. Yesterday, when you talked about me building muscle, it reminded me that Dad had said he'd get me weights when I turned twelve, and we'd work out together. Then he died, and now Mom's sad all the time and worried. She acts like she has to be both Mom and Dad to me."

He stared into his memories, "You know what I miss the most about dad being gone? Every night, after I was in bed, I could hear them in their bedroom talking over their day and laughing about things that happened. I couldn't hear what they were saying; it was just the comfort of their voices and their shared laughter. It made me feel safe and warm."

He felt the Holy Spirit impressing on him to talk to Zach, but he resisted. *What do I know that could help him?* Realizing that when God wanted you to do something, it was best to just go ahead and do it, he breathed a prayer for wisdom and tried, "You know Zach, you're carrying a lot of stuff that God wants to carry for you. It's okay to be sad that your dad died, but everything you've done to change yourself is only surface. Only God can heal the hurt inside you."

A choking sound was his only response, so he continued, "The other thing you need to know is that it's okay for men to grieve. There's nothing wimpy about crying."

A dam burst and Zach's shoulders were shaken with huge sobs. He cried and cried. Deke put an arm around him held him tightly, his eyes filling with tears at the boy's pain.

After a few moments, the flood ended, "Come on," he stood to his feet, dislodging a comatose Woofer, "your mom is waiting anxiously by the phone for me to call and say you've been found. If I don't get you home pretty soon, she's going to call out the National Guard."

They crawled out of the hideout and, brushing themselves off, headed toward his house. "Where's your phone?" he asked curiously. He didn't know for sure if Zach had a cell phone, but going by Chloe's usual indulgence, he expected that he did.

"I forgot to stick it in my pocket when I changed clothes after church."

"Not good, man. You need to be accessible to your mom. I imagine that is why she gave it to you, not so you could hone your Tetris skills." Giving in to an impulse, he grabbed Zach in a headlock and dragged him to his pickup, Zach laughing and Woofer running alongside barking in excitement, "Climb in, I'll get you home before your mom calls out the militia."

When they pulled into the driveway a couple of minutes later, Chloe catapulted off the steps. "Zacheus Phillip Evans, where have you been? Why didn't you take your phone? You are re-grounded; I have been worried out of my mind." Her voice trailed off when he stepped into the light. She could see that he had been crying.

He hugged her, "I'm sorry Mom, I just forgot the time," before heading on up the steps.

She swiveled back to face Deke, standing quietly to the side. "What happened? Was he hurt?"

He shook his head. "No, he was just revisiting how sad he was without his dad. I think his friends showed him how different his life used to be, and it opened up old hurts."

Chloe nodded, tears too close to allow her to speak, "Well," she swallowed, "thank you for finding him for me. Where was he?"

"He and his buds were at the park originally, but he'd gone back to the abandoned fort to be alone when it hit him."

"Thank you," she whispered.

"You're welcome, Chloe, he's really a good kid. Just keep being there for him, and he'll be fine." He resisted an urge to run his hand down her cheek.

She hesitated then asked diffidently, "Would you like a cup of coffee?"

She didn't need to be alone, her emotions were too vulnerable, and so he said easily, "Sure, I'd love a cup."

She led the way to the downstairs kitchen and made coffee, staring out the window while it bubbled and brewed. When finished she poured each of them a mug, and they sat at the table.

"A family is so fragile," she might have been talking to herself. He waited. She lifted her head and looked at him, "I feel like God has cheated me and Zach, but Zach most of all. Phillip was a very hands-on dad. He adored Zach, just like I did. It was so important to him to be there for him. Every spare moment he had, he spent with Zach, took him everywhere he went. Sounds like he was a dad more than a husband, but he wasn't. Anyway, I guess we both believed that kids need time with their parents, so we usually took him wherever we went, except for one night a week.

"Once a week, Phillip and I went out together, alone." She smiled at the memory, "Our date night." Her mouth tipped up at the corner, and she looked at Deke, "Zach gagged anytime he heard Phillip ask where I wanted to go on our date."

Deke smiled back, "He may have gagged, but trust me, he was pretty happy you two loved each other. I heard a saying once, 'The best thing a father can do for his kids is to love their mother.' I never forgot it because even though I never experienced it myself, I understood immediately the security that would come to children from a strong marriage. So be glad you had a happy marriage."

"Actually, happy marriages run in our family. There hasn't been a divorce in the McKinnon family as far back as we have records."

"Wow." He was quiet contemplating such an unusual statistic given the high divorce rate in American families. He wondered if it would qualify for the Guinness Book of World Records.

"Can't say all of them were blissful; however," Chloe continued, "I'll bet that if they were serious enough to remain in the marriage, they were probably serious about solving the problems, and maybe they became happily married."

He nodded, still trying to get his mind around a family that was totally intact for generations. He wasn't sure he had known any. His foster parents, David and Bea were one couple whose marriage had remained solid, but he knew for a fact that they had children that had divorced.

Chloe was continuing, "We have a pact in our family that everyone takes when they marry, which is to use the family as the first line of defense when a marriage runs into trouble. No guilt, no blame, just a whole bunch of people very convinced that problems can be solved and willing to help you figure it out and pray with you while you're going through it."

He felt something inside his chest wrench at her sadness and without thought slipped an arm around her shoulder, hugging her close, "I know you're sad and worried, but even in the few weeks I've known you and Zach, I've seen his attitude becoming better. You have lots to be thankful for, and you need to continue to pray for Zach's and your continued healing." She smiled and nodded.

He released her and took a step toward the door, "See you in the morning," and he shut her in and himself out and went home.

Chapter 13

About three o'clock Tuesday afternoon, he realized he was short a few bolts and got into his truck to run to the hardware store.

As he cruised down Beron, a figure darted into the street from between the cars and ran right in front of his truck. He stood on his brakes, his truck halting mere feet from the boy. Zach recognized him first, scrambling around the side of the truck and yanking on the door. Deke reached across and shoved the passenger door open, and Zach all but fell into the seat.

A commotion on the sidewalk brought Deke's eyes up, and he looked into the faces of a group who, judging by their angry words and gestures, had been chasing Zach. He gave them a level look and put the truck into gear, as Zach ducked down below the window, grabbing his seatbelt and fastening it.

They drove for a few blocks in silence, Deke allowing Zach time to gather himself before he started questioning him. Something was going on, and he needed to get to the bottom of it.

"You want to tell me what's going on?"

Zach opened his mouth, stopped, shut it, and sat mute. Deke's quick glance told him Zach was wrestling with something big. After moment, Zach said, "I went to the skateboard park, but no one was there. So I decided to drop by your house. I thought you'd be home from work by now, but cutting through the back, I found those guys had taken it over and didn't want me there."

Deke knew there had to be something more to the story. It was obvious, even though Zach wasn't going to admit it, that he had gone to the hide-out his mom had categorically said he was to stay away from. He hated being lied to, but he sensed that Zach might be willing to talk, and he didn't want to say anything to stop him. He decided to shelve the visit to the hardware store and go past his house to see if there was any evidence the gang might have left behind.

Zach resumed, "They were really jumpy, looking all around as if they didn't want to be seen. Something didn't feel right, and Mom doesn't want me going there anyway"—this with a virtuous air that made Deke wish that Zach was his kid so he could thump some sense into him—"so I began to leave, but I evidently made a noise, and they began to chase me." He was silent, looking out the window so Deke couldn't see his face. "I didn't stick around. When they came after me, I threw my skateboard at the first guy and beat feet." He hunched his shoulder, obviously hoping Deke wouldn't see the tremors in them, "Boy, am I glad you showed up."

"Did you recognize anyone?"

After a moment, Zach mumbled, "Like I said, they aren't school kids."

"Do you think they were doing drugs?"

"I didn't stick around."

Deke felt something off about Zach's response, but it could have been just adrenalin from being chased by a gang of thugs. More quietly he asked, "How long have you known my back property is being used by druggies?"

"No! I didn't know about it," Zach's eyes got wild like a rogue horse. "Remember, Mom won't let me hang around there anymore. I've never seen those older guys, but they were mad I'd seen them. They were running after me when I swerved in front of your truck and almost got hit before I realized it was you."

Deke was concerned about the potential for violence surrounding this kid and his way of relating a story without telling everything he knew. If he found out that Zach was into drugs, the fat was going to hit the fire. Until he had a little time to sort it out in his own mind, though, he wasn't going to approach Chloe, because as far as he could tell, Zach didn't show any signs of drug use.

He pulled into his lot, parked his truck, and opened the door, "Let's go see if your skateboard's still there."

He took a few steps before realizing Zach was still in the truck. He walked to Zach's side and spoke through the open window, "Come on." He hesitated offering Zach reassurances of safety for fear of offending him, but after a moment's long look in his face, Zach got out. They headed toward the back of the property, Zach velcroed to his back pocket. They found nothing. The barren area in the bushes was vacant. No trace remained of anyone having been there.

They were silent on the drive to The Perfect Child. Deke knew that Chloe had to be told, "Your mom needs to be told about this today."

"No way!" Zach was appalled. "She will freak out. I'll be grounded again, and I didn't do anything wrong!"

"She is your mother; I will not be a party to keeping her in the dark about something that has the potential to harm you."

Zach slammed back against the bench seat, crossing his arms, "You're going to tell her, then, because

I'm not saying anything," his jaw was firm.

Deke pulled in behind The Perfect Child, set the brake, and shifted to face Zach, still slouched against the door, "Zach, you happened to be in the wrong place at the wrong time, and if they are dealing drugs, you are in danger. Come on, we will both go tell you mom about it and see what she thinks should be done."

He opened the back door, Zach dragging behind like the downed tail of a kite. Chloe was wiping off counters, the sounds of kids playing formed a background, but she was alone in the day care kitchen. She turned to see who was at the door, and her eyes opened wide, "What happened?" She twisted her head to look around Deke, "Zach, what's going on?"

Deke shifted to one side, placed a hand on Zach's shoulder and gently urged him forward, "Zach happened onto a potentially bad situation this afternoon that you need to hear about." He nodded to Zach who grudgingly coughed up the story.

"I saw some guys at Deke's today doing a drug buy. They saw me watching and tried to catch me, but Deke drove by and picked me up." Chloe's eyes got bigger with each sentence.

When he finished she was uncharacteristically silent for a moment. Finally, she looked at Deke, "Should I call the police?"

He nodded. "Yes, I think we need to give them a heads-up. Although, since Zach can't identify anyone, I could call on my behalf and leave Zach out of it." Zach turned a hopeful face to his mom, but as soon as he caught her expression, he knew that wasn't going to fly.

"No, maybe Zach, with the help of a sketch artist, can help identify them if the police are interested." She walked to the wall and picked up the phone book on the shelf next to it. She looked up a number, dialed, and spoke into the receiver, "I need to report an incident this afternoon involving my son and what appeared to be a drug deal he stumbled on to." She turned from the phone, dug her hands in the back pockets of her jeans, and said, "An officer should be here within an hour to take his statement."

His admiration for her just kept rising. She truly was a straight arrow. Her kid would turn out fine with her as an example. He shifted for a moment, contemplating returning to work until the police arrived. "Well, then," he shifted on his feet. No sense heading to the hardware store again, he'd continue with something else, "I'll get back to work. Call me when they arrive."

Distracted she nodded, and didn't say anything when Zach followed Deke back outside. As soon as they were away from the house, Deke turned to face Zach, "You want to come clean about what you were really doing at the fort today? You were not coming to see me."

Zach fidgeted and shrugged, then finally heaved a big sigh, "I know Mom told me to stay away, but I had heard that someone might be selling drugs. Some of the kids are good guys, and I wanted to warn them not to go back to the fort. When they weren't at the park, I thought I'd just drop by the old fort really quick and give them a heads up and leave." His eyes met Deke's, "I am not doing drugs, that's just plain stupid. It's just," he hesitated, "they were the only kids who were friendly to me when I first moved here, and I thought I owed them."

Deke sighed, now it was his turn to hesitate. Maybe Zach was telling the truth and was concerned for his friends. He reached a decision, "I do not want to be put in the position to either keep something from your mom that she has a right to know or to rat on you.

Therefore, when you get home from school tomorrow, I expect you to be able to tell me that you told your mom that you visited the fort today and why you did it. Okay?"

Zach dropped his eyes. "Okay, you're right. I will. I promise."

"Good, how about helping me stack that lumber alongside the house so I can grab it more easily when I lay the floor tomorrow?" They spent the next hour completing this task.

###

The police arrived at 5:15 and spent an hour with all three of them. They had Zach repeat his story several times, taking down descriptions of the people he'd seen. Deke could tell by their questions they thought Zach knew more than he was saying, but they didn't push. They also didn't say anything about using a sketch artist, and no one suggested it to them.

After Chloe returned from escorting them to the door, Zach asked, "Can Deke stay for supper? That's meatloaf I smell isn't it?"

She was surprised at his request and judging by the expression on Deke's face, so was he, "Deke is welcome to eat with us." She looked at him.

He hesitated for moment, "Meatloaf, huh? Does she make a good one? I'm kind of a connoisseur."

Zach grinned, "She makes the best meatloaf in the world."

Deke stroked his chin, considering, "Well, okay, guess I ought to try it then."

She rolled her eyes, "Don't put yourself out on my account," and he grinned.

Fifteen minutes later found Zach setting the table

and Chloe dishing up the dinner. As they took their places, Deke held Chloe's chair for her. She didn't appear the least big discomfited by his manners; she simply spread her napkin in her lap, and under her steady gaze, so did Zach.

"Zach, do you want to pray for the meal?"

He bowed his head, "Thank you God for Mom's meatloaf and for Deke eating with us. Bless our food." He hesitated and Deke peeked at his face, before Zach added, "And God, thank you for having Deke close by to save me this afternoon. Amen."

The meal was as delicious as Zach promised, and Deke sincerely complemented her, "This is wonderful, Chloe, thank you for inviting me." They each concentrated on their plates the first few minutes. Along with a truly flavorful meatloaf, she had baked potatoes, steamed crisp snow peas, and hot crescent rolls. At the end of the meal, Deke was surprised when Zach rose without any prompting and cleared the table. Chloe got up and dished up bowls of cherry chip ice cream and homemade chocolate chip cookies.

"Yea, for baking day," Zach bit blissfully into a cookie.

Deke and Zach talked about skateboarding. At one point, Zach grumbled about needing a new skateboard because "now I don't even have my old skateboard."

"Maybe it will turn up; they may have dropped it alongside the road, and you'll find it in the next day or two," Chloe encouraged him.

Now Deke asked, "Why don't you build your own?"

"Build one? Guess I never thought of it. Wonder what it would cost?" Zach appeared caught by the possibility. A protest arose in Chloe's throat, but was never voiced. Why would she complain about her son creating something at home, where she would be able to see him more?

"How much do you think the materials would cost?" she turned to Deke.

"Hard, to tell, but if Zach would draw what he wanted, with the approximate dimensions, I could get a close enough figure to work with."

Zach shoved his chair back so quickly it flipped over. "I'll get a pad." He returned in less than a minute and sat back down, this time beside Deke. Just like that, she was excluded. The men pulled their chairs up to the table, the open notebook before them, pencils in hand, and commenced planning.

She sat in silence watching them for a few minutes. Finally, she smiled to herself, rose quietly, and left the room. Two hours later, she interrupted them, "Zach, tomorrow is still a school day. If you guys call it quits for tonight, Deke can come over tomorrow for dinner, too, if you need more planning."

Deke stretched and glanced at the clock on her wall. "Wow, can't believe it's that late. How about if I take you out for supper tomorrow night—how does Zeeks sound?"

"Really great," Zach crowed. He and Chloe both loved Zeek's pizza. Deke eyed Chloe, "Are you for it?"

She smiled, "I love Zeeks. We'd love to go."

Zach disappeared to his room, and Chloe walked Deke downstairs to let him out. The tension between them seemed to have risen during the evening. She felt adrenalin surge through her veins and wondered if he could tell she was tense.

With his hand on the doorknob, he turned to face her. Before she was aware of her intention, she reached up, grasped Deke's face between her hands, and directed it down to her mouth. She kissed him soundly, and a moment later, he took the initiative from her, pulled her close and kissed her back. Thoroughly. When they broke apart, they gazed, almost in shock, into each other's eyes.

"Well," Chloe breathed, "now we know."

Deke observed her with a baffled expression, rubbed his face, and murmured, "Yeah, I guess we do." In a daze he got into his pickup and went home.

###

Something woke her. Chloe sat up in bed and looked around, confused as to why she would be awake. She rolled over and looked at the glowing hands of the clock on her bedside table. It read 3:08. What had she heard? She swung her legs over the side of the bed and walked to the windows overlooking the front of the house. All was dark and quiet on the street. Too early even for the newspaper boy to be delivering. Uneasy, she walked through the apartment living room and into the kitchen, to check out the window that looked out onto the back of the property. The kitchen window was cracked, allowing a couple of inches of cool air to flow in and, along with it, the sound of scrabbling and low whispers. Someone was at her downstairs' back door trying to get inside!

Stealthily she backed up until her back hit the door jam, and her arm reached for the wall phone hanging beside it. When she discovered the line was dead, her blood congealed and she realized they were in serious trouble. Instinctively she raced on bare feet to her bedroom, scrambled for her purse, and her cell phone in the front pocket. Her hands were trembling so much she had a hard time flipping up the lid. She hit 9-1-1. The dispatcher's voice asked her the nature of her problem, and she whispered furiously, "Someone is breaking into my house!"

"Just stay calm ma'am. What is your address?"

She quietly gave it, adding, "Please hurry!" Then she gasped, "Oh, my son. I've got to get my son!"

"Ma'am, do not hang up," the voice instructed her. "Go get your child, and both of you go into the safest room of the house. The police are on their way."

She raced out of her room, almost bouncing off Zach's door as she wrenched it open. "Zach, Zach!" her whisper brought him upright out of a sound sleep. "What...?" his question was interrupted by the sound of breaking glass downstairs and then the noise of running feet leaving the property, headed toward the alley. A moment later there was loud banging on the front door, and a voice shouted, "Police! Open up!"

Relieved that rescue had arrived, she unlocked their apartment and raced down the dark stairs to open the front door. She noticed the strong smell of gasoline as she made her way to the door. She wondered where it could have come from as she opened the front door to a uniformed cop. Another of Seattle's best appeared in the doorway of the day care kitchen behind her.

Confused, she looked between the two officers. The one in the kitchen held out a glass jar with a rag hanging out of it and spoke to his partner, "We arrived just in time. They were about to throw in a Molotov cocktail when they heard us arrive."

Chloe felt the strength leave her legs, and she propped herself up on the wall of the entry. "Who would try and burn down my house?"

The officer faced her, "Do you have anyone who

has a grudge against you? Have you had problems with your neighbors or anything that could explain this?"

Before she could answer, Zach crept into the room in flannel pajama pants, his bony chest bare, and his hair all rumpled, "Mom, are you all right? What happened?"

The policeman turned to him, "You are?"

"Zach Evans," he stammered. He pointed, "That's my mom." Then noticing the object in the officer's hand, he approached, "What's that?"

"It appears to be a homemade firebomb. We interrupted someone from launching this into your house. Would you know anything about this?"

"No," Zach noticed his skeptical look and insisted, "no, of course not," indignantly. Then he sobered, "Well unless those guys found out where I live."

She explained to the officer's questioning look, "I filed a report about some young men trying to beat up my son. Zach happened on to what appeared to be a drug buy."

The policeman noted it in his notebook, "We'll look into it, but what about anyone else? Maybe someone who could be mad at him and retaliating for something?"

Chloe shrugged, "It's anybody's guess what could be happening. I know some of them are pretty rough. And since Zach has stopped hanging around with them, they seem to take it personally. So yes, I guess it might be former friends of his."

The police stayed to help them cover the broken window. From the wood pile one of them found a suitable board, but Chloe didn't even own a hammer, and Deke certainly hadn't left one of his.

She was close to losing it when Deke pulled into

the yard. He got out, holding his tool belt. She gazed at him in astonishment, aware that the tension thrumming inside stilled as soon as she saw him. He introduced himself to the officers, conferred with them for a moment, and then taking the board the officer held, strode toward the back door.

"How did you get here?" After all that had happened in the past hour, Chloe was beyond surprise anymore.

"Zach called," Deke said briefly around a nail in his mouth as he positioned the board. Two swift thuds later, the door was once again secure. He turned to look at her, "Are you all right?"

She nodded in bemusement. "They think TJ or one of his friends is retaliating."

Just then the police interrupted to say goodbye. "Here is my card," the officer in charge handed her a piece of cardboard. "We may be back tomorrow with more questions." He handed her some papers, "Here is our report, and this," he pointed to a number in the upper right corner of the page, "is the case number. If you have anything to add or any questions, give this number to the duty officer, and he will know which case to bring up."

Zach crept out on the sunroom floor as they left, looking first at his mom then at Deke. "Thanks, for coming," he said awkwardly, eyeing his mom as if unsure of her reaction.

She smiled tiredly at Deke, 'Yes, thank you for helping us out. I appreciate it."

Deke nodded soberly, "I don't imagine they'll be back again, at least tonight, but if you're uneasy, I'll be glad to sleep on the playroom couch." He grimaced, "I don't believe I'd fit on one of the cots."

Zach snorted, envisioning Deke's length laid out accordion fashion on a preschool cot.

Chloe smiled too, "No, thanks for the offer, but I agree there's probably not any danger tonight. Let's just all go back to bed and try this night again."

Deke nodded then turned to Zach, "Make sure you check all the doors and windows downstairs to make sure none of them have been compromised, and be sure to bolt the door on the stairs to your apartment." Chloe watched Zach grow visibly taller at Deke's instructions. He awkwardly held out his hand, and they shook solemnly, "I will, man. I'll take care of her."

She smiled and turned to go inside. Being a mom, if she didn't disappear, she'd say something foolhardy like, "I'll make sure everything is secure," and end up ruining this coming-of-age ritual she knew instinctively was important for Zach.

As he promised, Zach toured the downstairs making sure everything was secure, and bolted the door on the stairs before turning toward the apartment. "I'm pooped," he declared, striding toward his bedroom and well-earned rest from a long day of defending his family.

Chloe headed to her bed and to what she thought would be three hours of tossing and turning and was asleep the minute her head hit her pillow.

Chapter 14

Over the next few days Chloe contemplated the affect Deke was having on her family. She tried not to let her mind dwell on the sweetness of his kiss; that would be just too much temptation. After talking with him about her over-involvement and the problems with Zach, she had begun to implement the changes she had felt were needed.

She was in the process of hiring a second teenager to help Tasha in the afternoon. This would free her to leave every day at four p.m. Now, knowing that she would be free, Zach had promised to be home by five. Even now he usually returned before then and was doing his homework on his laptop at the kitchen table when she came upstairs to cook supper.

Against her wishes, her mind seemed determined to dwell on Deke's kiss and the electricity it had generated between them. He hadn't kissed her again, and she was alternately disappointed and relieved. She wasn't sure if starting a second relationship was a wise thing for her. Raising a teen was hard enough without adding a stepfather to the mix – not that Deke gave any indication that he was in the running for such a position.

She had discussed her confusion with Maddie who had advised, "You have had a lot of changes to deal with. Let this one develop on its own and see where it goes." She had decided that was wise, and relaxed.

###

Out in the backyard, Zach obviously had something on his mind. Finally, after watching him start and stop several simple chores, Deke couldn't stand his fidgeting any longer and demanded, "What's the matter? Did something happen at school that you need to talk about?"

"What?" Zach looked at him, "Oh," his face reddened, and he looked down at his feet. "Sorry, um," he hesitated, "can I ask you something?"

"Yes," Deke eyed him warily. "You can ask, but I won't promise an answer. It depends on the question."

"Do you like my mom?" he blurted.

"Yes, I like your mom, fine."

"I mean, like, uh, like someone you'd like to date."

It was certainly something he had considered a lot lately, but he wasn't about to talk about it with a thirteen-year-old. "Why do you want to know? Are you going to warn me to stay away from her?"

"No, I mean," it burst from him in a rush, "I like you. You're a good guy, and I think my mom needs someone like you. The thing is," he continued confidentially, "she seems really rude and stuff, but she's really not." Deke didn't say anything and Zach plunged on, "She's actually a lot of fun once you get to know her. She's just had to be tough because Dad died, and she had to begin a business, and she's worried about taking care of me."

"Well, you're not acting like so much of a stinker anymore; she should be relaxing," Deke said.

"Oh, she's mellowing, but I think it's your influence not mine."

"Hmmm."

"So?"

He glanced at him, "So? I may be thinking of asking your mother for a date, but I assure you, I will talk with her before I tell you about it. Now get over here and help me." It must have satisfied Zach because he grinned happily.

Chloe was folding laundry in the downstairs laundry room when Deke entered through the back door.

"Hi," she said eyeing him, uneasy about the gleam in his eye. "Did you need something?" For some reason he was making her nervous. It was probably herself; the more time she spent with him, the more attracted she was. There were so many things about him that were attractive.

He stood in the doorway, a slight grin on his face, "Your son thinks I ought to ask you out on a date."

She dropped the towel she was folding and stared at him, her throat dry, "H-he does?"

"Hmm, I hadn't asked you earlier because I wasn't sure if he was ready to see his mom go out with another man, even casually." He seemed suddenly unsure, "Would you like to go out?"

A big smile crossed her face, "Yes, I'd like that very much. When?"

He was relieved she could tell, "How about Friday night after you close? I happen to know that the youth group is going to a hockey game. Is Zach going along?"

"Yes, he has to be at the church at five-thirty."

"Okay, if I pick both of you up at five-fifteen, we can drop Zach off and go on to dinner from there." She was still smiling. She was beautiful, and he was aware that he was grinning back at her like a loon.

"Will it be casual or dressy?"

See? That's why he hated dating. How did he know the difference between casual and dressy. Maybe if he told her the restaurant, she'd be able to gauge. "Do you like Pacific Rim cuisine?"

"Love it," she assured him.

"Then let's go to the Pacific Pearl. Mrs. Watanabe tells me it's as close to authentic as we get here.

By the time the day ended on Friday, she was a bundle of nerves. *What was I thinking?* her mind shrieked as she stood in front of her closet and contemplated clothing choices. She actually considered calling Deke and canceling, but knowing he would tease her kept her from carrying it out. Finally, she settled on one of her favorite dresses, a navy blue sheath in light wool with a softly-draped cowl neck. She threaded dangly earrings of Austrian crystal suspended from delicate silver chains in her ears, picked up a light wool shawl to throw over her arms, and slid a small, black silk purse on a velvet strap over her shoulder. She had heard the doorbell a moment ago, and as she walked towards the living room, she hoped it wasn't raining because she still hadn't invested in a dressy raincoat—a silly oversight in a city known for its rain.

When she walked into the living room, Deke and Zach were standing by the door waiting and talking about skateboarding. Deke had on dress slacks, a dark brown shirt, and a brown-on-brown silk tie; she was glad she had taken pains with her appearance. Distracted he broke off mid-sentence, watching her approach, and it was obvious by the darkening of his eyes he liked what he saw. He finally found his voice as she reached him and took her shawl from her, draping it over her shoulder, saying prosaically, "Are you ready?" But she wasn't fooled, she had seen the look in his eyes, and she suddenly felt excited about her evening out.

They dropped Zach off in the church parking lot, and Deke asked the Olsen's if they'd mind dropping him back home. Mr. Olsen grinned at both of them and slapped his hand on Deke's back, "Be glad to," he beamed.

"Well, that was subtle," Deke muttered as he shifted into drive and pulled out of the lot. Chloe felt a bubble of laughter rise in her throat; it had been a long time since she had felt carefree. He glanced at her as she laughed, and she turned her head to meet his eyes, "I feel great," she beamed, " I feel alive."

His anxiety melted at the sheer joy reflecting in her face. He grinned back and pushed down on the accelerator, "Happy, huh?" He reflected for a moment, then nodded, "So am I. Thanks for coming out with me. And in case I haven't said it, you look fantastic."

The drive to the restaurant was a matter of minutes, and in a short time they were walking into the elegant lobby. She had felt tall in her four-inch heels, but beside her, Deke still towered. He gave his name for their reservation, and a moment later an elegant blonde in a drop-dead gorgeous black sheath escorted them to a table with a window view of Lake Union.

She examined the beautiful room—cedar beams spanned the ceiling, the walls not filled with glass were paneled in rough cedar, and framed watercolors of the Northwest hung on the walls. Underneath their feet the teak floor was polished to a rich glow. One side of the restaurant was a sushi bar, the black wood gleaming under the low lights illuminating the diners.

Deke nodded his head, "Sushi?"

She shook her firmly. "No, never have cared for it, sorry."

"Don't be. I love it, but since I've eaten Mrs. Watanabe's, I'm not interested in having it in a restaurant. I'm afraid it won't measure up."

"Mrs. Watanabe?"

"My neighbor, who feeds me several times a week. She and her husband ran a Chinese restaurant for years, even though they're Japanese, and she's got an amazing talent for cooking."

The tables were covered in salmon linen and the linen napkins were a deep rust. The chair Deke held for her was polished black wood with a ladder back and leather seat

"Have you been here before?" She inquired as she opened the heavy leather-bound menu the hostess handed her.

"No, I'm just hoping their food lives up to their reputation." He scanned the selections. "How about an appetizer?"

"Sounds good. I will probably enjoy everything except calamari."

"Escargot?"

"If the spices are right, I love it."

"Okay, then." He looked more closely at the appetizers, "Let's don't try and decide on one thing." He looked up at their waiter, "We'll have the Asian Lily Appetizer Platter."

After the waiter had taken the rest of their order and departed, she took a deep breath and let it out. "This is wonderful. It's been a long time since I've gone out without family and all dressed up too. Thank you so

Comment [JSS]: Are you holding a place here for the platter name?

much, Deke."

His smile was warm and infectious, "Long time for me too. It's too easy to get busy making a living and forget that adding relaxation to your life is really important. Thank you for coming with me."

They talked about anything and everything, changing subjects easily as they dined on Green Papaya Salad, prawns, and Chicken Pad Thai.

The restaurant was elegant, and there was a beautiful view of the Seattle lights from their window table. Deke had been more adept with chopsticks than she, and they laughed companionably at her attempts.

"Had to learn," he confided, "Mrs. Watanabe wasn't about to allow any of those metal implements into her kitchen, and her cooking is too good to pass up. I practiced until I was able to even scoop rice in my mouth without it landing in my lap."

Through their conversation, they discovered they had quite a lot in common – they were conservative in their approach to life and business, believed their relationship with God was the cornerstone of their lives—not just a Sunday observance—and enjoyed books over movies or television. They had finished the evening strolling around the Seattle Center, watching the water in the fountain and listening to the music piped out of the speakers. He walked her up the stairs to her apartment just before eleven o'clock and kissed her gently before leaving.

###

On Monday Chloe contemplated her weekend. Mondays were her favorite day of the week. She loved the clean slate that a new week brought, and she always started each one full of optimistic plans. No one was sick, neither child nor worker, and the day proceeded smoothly. Seemed like a good time to remember her *date.*

Maria and Mrs. Thompson, even Tasha, knew she had gone out with Deke on Friday. They had smiled knowingly at her all day, aware that her smile kept breaking through at odd moments, but none of them teased her about it.

She was in the kitchen about four p.m., and as she pushed open the window to allow the sweet breeze in, she heard snatches of Zach and Deke's conversation. A moment later, her attention was grabbed when she heard Zach say, "… they pretty much leave me alone. They still think I ratted them out." He must have noticed the underlying sadness in his tone because he shifted his voice to full bravado, "But I don't care. Let them think whatever they want, they're just jerks."

"Yes they are, not only for blaming you for something without any proof and not believing you when you tell them the truth, but also for breaking the law to begin with. We'd have a pretty chaotic society if everyone broke any law they considered stupid or unnecessary."

Deke changed the subject, "So, we need to get busy on that skateboard."

"Yes, but just as soon as I settle on a design, I think of something else, and it changes."

"I went online last night and looked up that Hawk guy you talked about." Never by a tone of his voice did he give away that he had already heard of Tony Hawk. Chloe's heart warmed at his kindness in not taking away a young kid's thunder. "Anyway, you've got good instincts for woodworking; I've seen that in the past few weeks."

"I do?" Zach couldn't have sounded prouder if Deke had told him that he thought Zach was able to turn water into wine.

When the last child left for the day, she opened the back door to tell Zach she was going upstairs to fix dinner and impulsively asked, "Deke, would you like to stay and eat with us?"

He nodded, "I never turn down good food, especially food I don't have to cook. I'd love to. Will I have time to take Woofer home and get cleaned up?"

"You bet, but Woofer can come upstairs and keep me company while I cook." At his name, the Airedale lifted his head from where he'd been lounging on the sun porch. He stretched and yawned then ambled over to her.

"Poor baby," she crooned, "the kids wore you out at the park today, didn't they?" Woofer panted in happy agreement. "You come upstairs with Chloe, and I'll let you have a treat." She had bought dog biscuits last week so the kids could give Woofer a couple each day, and she snagged a few as she headed toward the stairs, Woofer padding along behind.

Maleficent, who had the run of the whole building, had already met Woofer and, realizing he wasn't going away, had settled for regal shunning. When he entered the apartment she opened one eye from her doze on the sofa then turned her head away and ignored him. Woofer happily headed toward her, but a word from Chloe brought him back in line to follow her to the kitchen.

Forty minutes later, Zach came up to shower and change, telling her Deke had said he'd only be a few minutes. Just before seven all three sat down at the table. Chloe shook out her napkin, raising her eyebrows at her son, who hastily set down his glass of milk and picked up his napkin and placed it in his lap, grinning as he did so.

She turned to Deke, "Would you like to ask the

blessing tonight?"

He nodded, "Be glad to. Dear Jesus, thank you for the delicious meal that Chloe has prepared and the friendship of Chloe and Zach. We thank you for all the blessings you have given us and praise you for them. Amen."

They were busy passing chicken-fried steak, mashed potatoes, gravy, and green beans. After a few minutes of silent consumption, Deke spoke to Zach, "Why don't you get busy and finish your sketch for a new board. Once it's finished we can get onto the more fun task of tracking down the materials you'd need."

Zach pushed back his chair, went to his room, and returned with a sketchpad, that Chloe and Deke could see was full of sketches of skateboards, ramps, and wheels—some in pencil, others in color. Chloe had no idea that he could draw like that. Deke took it from him, and thumbed through the pages. Zach hung excitedly over his shoulder, "See the problems I'm having? Too many choices: This one is made from wood and had acrylic wheels. This is fiberglass. I've heard that fiberglass isn't hard to work with, but I don't know all the materials I'd need. I could look it up on Google though."

Deke, who hadn't said anything, now spoke, "I've got a lot of usable supplies at my place. These are really good Zach. You not only have an artist's eye, you have a good eye for scale." Zach flushed at the praise.

Chloe didn't interrupt them. They were once again totally engrossed in the sketches and plans. She stood and cleared the table, listening to them talk about the merits of hard plastic cores versus solid polyurethane wheels and fiberglass over wood. After about twenty minutes, Deke lifted his head, "Sorry, we forgot all about you. If you don't mind, Zach and I'll run out to my place and see what materials I have that he could use and maybe run by Home Depot and price some stuff. Would that be okay? You're welcome to come along."

Zach watched her hopefully. She knew that allowing him to go alone with Deke was his desire. "Take your phone so I can get a hold of you if I need to," he gave her a brilliant smile as she continued, "and be home by nine, you have school tomorrow."

"Yes, ma'am," he saluted her then grabbed his sketchbook and hurried out the door.

Deke stood and smiled at Chloe, "I'll take good care of him; I won't even take him on my Hog." He waited for her glare to materialize, which it did, then grinned. "Thanks for dinner. It was delicious. Next time I'll make my famous flat iron steak dinner for us."

"You're welcome," she murmured. Her brows pleated in a frown as she thought about the ramifications of Deke and Zach spending free time together. She hadn't been looking for a relationship and wasn't sure if what she and Deke had could be construed as one, but somehow, without her being sure of how it had happened, Deke had become an important person to both her and Zach. She could tell from the gleam in his eye that he could accurately read her expression. She wiped all expression from her face and added neutrally, "Drive carefully. He's very dear to me."

He nodded once, "Will do," and he followed Zach down the stairs and out.

###

On Friday afternoon, Chloe had just looked at the clock for the second time, wondering if she had forgotten that Zach had told her he had something he was going to do after school instead of coming straight home. Just then,

Tasha hurried in the door, her eyes huge in her face, "Miss Chloe, there's a policeman at the door asking for you." Chloe felt all the blood drain from her face at the same moment the back door opened and Deke's quiet voice said, "Police are here. What do they want?"

She turned to him, her eyes enormous in her small face, "I don't know. Oh, Deke, something has happened to Zach, I just know it." He reached her in two strides and slid a strengthening arm around her waist, "Hold on, we don't know anything, maybe Daniel took apart the street out front," but she was too terrified to smile at his sally. He urged her toward the front of the house, "Let's go find out."

"Mrs. Evans?" The officer stood inside the doorway, a dozen small inquisitive preschoolers eyeing him from their side of the room.

"Yes," she gulped, "has something happened to Zach? My son, Zach?" She was trembling so hard it was difficult to form the words. A feeling of dread settled over her, and doom filled her heart.

The policeman obviously knew to cut to the chase with parents because he stated succinctly, "Ma'am, if Zach Evans is your son, he has been in an accident, but he is okay. He has been taken to Harborview Medical Hospital, and you need to go there now."

She froze, staring up at him. No! She'd already lost Phillip; she couldn't lose Zach.

Deke shook her gently, "Chloe, listen to the man. Zach is not going to die."

She gathered herself and paid attention to what the officer was reporting, "…he was evidently beat up by a group of teens after school today. A parent passing by, after picking up her child at school, saw it happening. She stopped and yelled and the perpetrators ran off. She called 9-1-1, and Zach has been taken to Harborview Medical. If you need a ride, my partner and I are ready to take you to the hospital."

Deke interrupted, "There's no need. I'll drive her."

He turned to Tasha, who spoke up immediately, "Go on, Chloe, I'll wait until all the kids are gone; I'll lock up. Just please call and let me know how Zach is, okay?"

Mrs. Thompson standing behind her added, "I'll stay with her; don't worry about the business, we'll be fine."

In a daze, she was dimly aware of Deke stuffing her arms into a windbreaker, while Tasha grabbed her purse and looped it over her shoulder. Then he led her down the steps and to his truck. He opened the passenger door and urged her to climb up, reaching in to fasten her seatbelt before trotting around the hood of the truck, sliding behind the wheel, and starting the engine. The ride to the hospital was silent; Chloe stared straight ahead, finding it hard to even breath as fear threatened to overwhelm her. Deke was aware of her distress. He reached over and laid his big hand across her hands twisted together in her lap and clasped them gently without saying anything.

At the hospital, he pulled up to the emergency entrance and instructed, "Go on in. I'll park the truck and follow you immediately."

She hopped out, slammed the door, and tore into the reception. "My son, Zach Evans, was just brought in," she gasped to the woman in charge.

The receptionist, dressed in slacks, a bright pink blouse, and wearing half-glasses, looked at her computer screen and smiled, "He's fine, if you'll just sit down for a moment, we'll get you back there right away. The doctor's with him right now, and he will want to talk with you, too."

Chloe slid into a chair beside the registration desk, groped through her billfold for her insurance card, and answered the questions the woman asked her to complete the patient registration. Inside she was screaming at the delay, but she knew the sooner she cooperated, the sooner she would get to see her son.

In a very short time, Deke was there, standing solidly behind her chair, his presence a huge comfort to her. After signing all the paperwork, the clerk pushed a button, and the door leading into the Emergency Room itself swung open automatically. "Go straight in, he's in cubicle 2A. The rooms are marked, and it will be on the left-hand side, about halfway down."

Chloe was through the door before she finished her instructions, Deke right behind her. "Here," he gently urged her to turn, and they entered an examining booth. She saw Zach lying on the gurney looking small and obviously battered, and she burst into tears.

"Mom," he turned toward her, and she gathered him close. It was evident by his relaxing into her arms that he had been a very scared young man. She hugged him gently, afraid of causing more pain, because it was evident he was hurting and then set him away so she could look at him. "What happened?" Now that she could see for herself that he was alive and, while not fine, certainly not in any serious shape, she calmed down.

"Ma'am," she looked up and noticed for the first time that there was a police officer in the cubicle with him, "we need to ask Zach some questions but waited until you arrived for your permission to speak with him.

May I ask him about what happened?"

"Yes, yes, of course." She turned to Zach, "Tell us what happened."

He sat without speaking for a minute and then he lifted his eyes, not to her, but to Deke. He almost seemed to be begging forgiveness, "I thought I was doing the right thing," he pleaded. "They said if I'd just keep my mouth shut, they wouldn't hurt Mom, but when the police showed up at school today asking questions, they said I was the only one who could have talked. They were going to teach me a lesson."

Deke reached forward and laid a comforting hand on Zach's shoulder. "I'm sorry it happened, son," Chloe momentarily wondered if he was even aware what he had called Zach. "Unfortunately, standing up for what is right often causes us pain. We're proud you still chose to do right."

The officer now spoke, "Zach, the only way to stop them is for you to come clean about everything. Who are these people?"

Zach turned to him, "I don't know the new guys. They started hanging out at the skate park a few weeks ago, and TJ began boasting that he was going to be in a lot of money pretty soon. But they made me nervous the way they talked and it didn't take any brains to know that if you're making big money fast it has to involve drugs. I thought if I just ignored them I'd be fine. But there are guys at the park who admire TJ and buy into his bull, and I wanted to warn them, so I went back to the fort to warn them and instead stumbled onto TJ's first buy."

"That was when they were chasing you, and I happened by?" Deke inserted.

Zach nodded, "Deke rescued me; then that night

they threw a bomb into the house, and when TJ stopped me at school the next morning he said it was just a show of what they could do and 'wouldn't it be sad if Mom died?'" Zach took a big breath and resumed, "He promised me if I kept my mouth shut everything would be fine."

"Only Mom had mentioned TJ's name to the officers, and they followed up with him today, and everything fell apart."

The officer had been taking notes on his laptop while Zach spoke, and now he inquired, "Did you hear any names? Did someone address them in any way that you could ID them?"

Zach thought for a moment, "I heard one of them call the other one Paco."

He clicked a few more keys and then turned the laptop so that the screen faced Zach. "Paco Chavez, is this the man you saw with your friend?"

Zach scowled, "TJ's not my friend, and yes, that is the guy. How did you know him?"

The officer looked at Chloe and Deke, "He's affiliated with a drug cartel from Mexico. They're just moving into the area, and they are dangerous."

Chloe felt all the blood leave her face, "My son is known to a drug cartel?" she whispered.

Again the officer hit a few keys, and showed Zach a second photo, "This is his known sidekick, Miguel Ramirez, was he along?"

Zach nodded, "Yes, he was there too."

The policeman shut the laptop and stood up, "Okay, I think we have enough. When you're released, you will need to come down to the station and file a formal report and sign it. We will keep you informed of the progress we are making. I don't believe you're in any danger since they are probably lying low to regroup; however, keep your eyes peeled in the next few days for any unusual people or cars in your neighborhood."

Chloe stared at the back of the policeman as he exited then swung her horrified gaze to Deke's. Her eyes begged him for reassurance. Deke concerned gaze met hers.

Chloe finally gathered herself and asked Zach, "What does the doctor say about your injuries?"

A voice behind her answered, "Dr. Shaffer says this young man is lucky that someone happened by and rescued him."

They turned to see the physician standing inside their cubicle scanning Zach's paperwork. "No internal bleeding, that's good. Hmm, bruised ribs, choke marks on his neck, and it appears he wrenched his knee as he fought back. Good for you." He closed the file, "I am going to admit him for observation overnight. He took quite a blow to his head when they first took him down, and while it doesn't appear that he has a serious concussion, I would feel better keeping him for at least another twelve hours. The police have already informed us of the potential danger, and we have removed his name from the admitting records. A security guard will be in the hall all night."

Chloe nodded, "That's fine. I'll stay with him."

"No, Mom," the embarrassment in Zach's voice told her more than anything else that he was not seriously injured.

She had turned and pointed a finger at him to argue, when Deke reached over her shoulder and captured the finger inside his hand saying smoothly, "I'll just take her for some supper while they settle you into your room. Once she sees that you're doing fine I'm sure she'll agree to go home so that both of you can get some rest. Okay?"

They stood united in male solidarity, and Zach's look of gratitude to Deke spoke volumes, "Thanks."

"Okay, then" arm around her shoulder, Deke steered her out of the cubicle and through the waiting room. She didn't say anything until she was buckled in her seatbelt in his truck, and he had slid behind the wheel.

"Well, fine," she sounded grumpy because she was. Zach was her kid, and he was injured. Who was he to tell her what she should or should not do? If she wanted to stay with her son to make sure he was cared for during the night, neither Deke nor Zach were big enough to stop her.

Deke pulled into the parking lot of a Denny's close to the hospital and came around to help her alight. Once seated in a booth, and ordered, he glanced at her sitting ramrod straight, her mouth primed into a straight line.

"Okay, let me have it."

She sniffed, "I don't know what you mean." Before he could respond, she rushed on, "He's my son. He's been hurt, and I will spend the night, and you can't stop me."

He suppressed a grin, "Look, Chloe, I understand your terror and your desire to care for him, but he's almost fourteen. The last thing he wants is for his mom to take care of him." Her bottom lip simply stuck out farther. "How about if we eat, and both of us go back to the hospital until about ten o'clock. If he's not running a fever or showing any other adverse signs, I'll take you home so you can get a good night's sleep."

She didn't want to give up, "He's hurting; he won't be able to sleep. I should be there."

"Probably in a perfect world, you should, but in this world, adolescent males are very sensitive to appearing to need their moms. So give him a break. He probably will be miserable; he may even be glad you stayed at some point, but for the time being, he'll feel humiliated."

It was the prospect of humiliating her son that did it. She could relate to all the times that she'd felt humiliated by her mother's behavior. She didn't want Zach to have those memories himself. "Okay," grudgingly, "I'll just stay until he's settled, and then I will go home."

He patted her shoulder. "I know it's hard, but you're doing the right thing for him," he shifted for the waitress to place their plates in front of them and dropped the subject.

The evening progressed. Tasha arrived around seven, anxious for the full story. Chloe allowed Zach to tell it and answer all her questions. Then Andrew and Angela, plus their parents, arrived about seven-thirty. They had a mug holding a monster fashioned from a chrysanthemum, which made Zach laugh. The pastor from All Saints poked his head in, and it practically felt like a party. The pastor gathered everyone around the bed to thank God for Zach's escape and recovery. Looking at all their new friends, thanks to Deke, Chloe felt included as a part of a group for the first time since they had moved to Seattle.

By eight-thirty everyone had left. The nurse brought in some meds for Zach, adjusted his IV, and in a few moments, Zach drifted off into a light doze. Deke dimmed the lights, and he and Chloe sat side-by-side for over an hour, not saying anything, watching Zach drift into a deeper sleep.

At nine-thirty she stirred, "Okay, you're right. He's doing fine. You can take me home." She wrote a short note and propped it up on the bedside table for Zach, should he wake up, and they left the hospital.

Driving out of the hospital parking lot, Deke didn't take the exit she expected. He explained, "It wouldn't be proper for me to stay at your home, even downstairs. So I'm going to get Woofer to stay with you. A dog as big and loud as he is will deter anyone from entering."

She saw the wisdom of his remark and didn't argue. A few moments later, he turned up a driveway and parked in front of a large Craftsman house. "I'll be right back," he said and exited the truck. She waited quietly, wondering about the beautiful residence before her. Within moments, Deke and Woofer exited, Deke carrying a small bag and dog bed. Woofer pranced happily alongside, eager at the prospect of a treat. He bounded gracefully into the bed of the pickup while Deke lifted the bag over the tailgate and slid back behind the steering wheel.

At her house, Deke said, "I'll wait until I see you wave from the living room window." He unloaded Woofer and handed Chloe the bag, which she saw upon inspection held his food bowls and a ration of food for him. He bent his head and kissed her soundly then gently pushed open the door for her and Woofer to enter.

Upstairs she walked to the window, looking down to see Deke standing against his truck. He saluted her, then got into the vehicle and left. She fed Woofer, showed him his bed, and collapsed in hers. Maleficent, a tangle of sleek fur hardly moved as she slid under her sheet and passed out.

Chapter 15

Thurmond James Bassinger III's arrest made the Seattle P.I.'s front page. Deke brought in the paper when he appeared at seven the next morning, coming into the kitchen by the back door as she unlocked it. He unfolded the headlines and thrust the paper into her hand. With Zach's ID of him and several others as those who had beat him up, one of the lesser kids had spilled his guts and implicated TJ in the drug scene big time.

"Evidently," he drawled, "TJ is one scary silent-partner dude for the local school drug scene. We are very blessed that all he did was have the local mafia help him beat up Zach."

Her heart warmed at the *We* and she began reading. The farther she read into the story, the more the color drained from her face, until finally she quit and leaned dizzily against the counter as it all hit her, "Zach was associated with a drug dealer in our town?" she gasped. "Where have I been? How did this happen? How could this have happened? All he did was go to school and hang out at the skateboard park in the neighborhood." She was shrieking by the end of her questions.

"Like I said, you'd be better off letting Zach build his own park here at home so you could watch who he hung around with."

"I've got a business to run," she wasn't aware that tears were streaming down her face. "He's just thirteen years old. He's mouthy and doesn't want me around, but he's not a druggie. Where did he get involved with them?"

"At the skateboard park. It brought a lot of kids together and was a perfect place for TJ to peddle his wares. And no place is off limits to drugs anymore. You're not so old that you don't understand that."

Chloe was glad that today was Saturday. She didn't know what she would have done if it had been another work day. It felt like all she had done recently was take advantage of her helpers. They had taken up slack for her like troopers, but enough was enough and she was glad that she didn't have to ask for any special favors today. She figured that by the time Monday rolled back around, either Zach would be ready for school or feel well enough to be left alone during the day.

She looked at Deke again, aware of the uplift in her spirits at just seeing him. "I was going to make a pot of coffee. I might as well do it here if you want a cup before we go."

"That would be great." He hung his jacket over the back of the kitchen chair. With the light pouring in from the sun porch remodel, the kitchen already appeared much roomier and open, even without any remodeling here. He surveyed it with satisfaction. "Nothing better than feeling you've done a good job on something. And if I do say so myself, that sunroom is going to be a great addition to your space."

She turned, smiling, and handed him his mug, fixed just the way she'd seen him do it in the past months, "You can say it, and I'll still agree. I already love it. It's going to be warm and open, totally perfect to give the kids the feeling of freedom."

###

It was after two o'clock before they got Zach back

to the apartment. As per usual, the paperwork wasn't finished, and Chloe spent almost forty minutes waiting for the doctor to sign the release and for his instructions and the drugs Zach needed to be checked out to her.

Finally though, they were in the pickup, Chloe in the middle and Zach, dressed in the jeans and t-shirt she had brought with her, buckled up by the door.

As soon as they exited the parking lot, Deke leaned around her to asked Zach, "Hungry?"

"Hungry! Man, am I ever. Whatever that was on the plate at breakfast was gross. Please, can we stop and get a burger?"

Deke was already headed for the local drive-in close to the hospital. He pulled in under the awning and punched a button to give their order. "Zach?"

"Two double cheeseburgers, large fry and a large blackberry milkshake, please."

"Chloe?"

"I'll have a junior burger with everything, hold the onions, and a small Pepsi."

Deke relayed their order adding, "Plus another double cheeseburger, a large order of Tater Tots and a strawberry milkshake. Oh, and change that Pepsi to a raspberry milkshake. Okay?"

Chloe exclaimed, "Deke, I can't eat all that. I'm still stuffed from breakfast."

Deke snorted, "What breakfast? I'll bet it was a piece of toast, right?"

"That's okay, Mom," Zach was quick to help out, "whatever you don't finish, I will."

While they waited for their order, Deke said, "The paper says they arrested TJ last night on drug charges."

He waited for Zach's reaction.

Zach was quiet, internalizing the information, and then he turned to Deke, "I thought about what you said yesterday, about doing right? I guess I should have spoken up immediately. Some things are just too dangerous to keep quiet about." He reflected, "I needed to choose sides, huh?"

Deke nodded soberly, "Nothing destroys lives quicker than drugs."

Chloe felt anger roiling within her; all this was going on under the watchful eyes at Fowler Academy! The two overriding reasons most of the parents, herself included, chose to pay big bucks for a prestigious private school was a more challenging education and a supposedly better class of students. Ha! Before she could react though, Deke's leg gently nudged hers alongside his, and she calmed herself. Right now, Zach was willing to talk to Deke, and she just needed to listen.

She nodded in agreement, fighting the terror that threatened to engulf her. Her son was affiliated with a drug-running operation. So his acquaintance was a very small potato in the organization, it still chilled her to think of the kids he hung out with and how a very small shift could have lead him to follow in their footsteps. She swallowed hard and nodded again, not trusting her voice.

The carhop arrived just then with their food. The smells of onion and grilled meat fighting with hot potatoes revved up their taste buds. They quickly divided it up, Deke said a quick prayer of thanks for the food and for Zach's protection, and they dug in. To her surprise she ate every bit of her hamburger and part of Deke's tater tots, plus finished every drop of her shake.

Deke grinned as she handed him the trash, "Not hungry, huh?"

She paused in surprise, “Come to think of it, I didn’t eat any supper last night did I?”

“Well, you moved the food around your plate at Denny’s with great precision, but no one can fault you for not actually eating any Denny’s food. I should have taken you to a real restaurant.”

“I don’t think it would have helped. I was pretty upset last night.”

“Why?” Zach turned to her in honest bewilderment. Then at her snort of laughter, he looked to Deke for explanation.

Deke pulled Chloe close to his side and grinned, “Zach, for all we knew when a cop showed up on your mom’s doorstep last night, you could have been killed. Give her a break kiddo.”

“Oh,” he reflected for a moment then a grin broke out, “thought for a few minutes that I might be killed myself. I sure am glad Sarah’s mom stopped.”

Chloe stared at him, “What? You knew who stopped and helped you?”

“Yes, Sarah Kimble’s mom. Sarah was crying and everything.” He wavered between disgust at the display of emotion and secret elation that someone cute cared what happened to him.

Chloe frowned. Honestly, males! She said with great forbearance, “Thank you, Zach, for giving me a name. I need to call her and thank her for saving my son’s life.”

“Oh, yeah, guess that would be good.”

Deke picked up Zach Monday morning, and they paid a visit to the police station. Zach hadn’t mentioned what had transpired, but Deke had filled Chloe in at lunch, which somehow they seemed to share every day now.

"The officer was very thorough. He questioned Zach closely before he agreed that he wasn't involved in the drug dealing. He was very appreciative of the names Zach provided and promised to do his best to keep Zach's name out of the reports."

"So what now?" Chloe inquired. "I mean, obviously, Zach is not going back to the skate park."

"No," Deke nodded in agreement, "going back would not be a wise idea anymore. I guess you're going to have to go forward and allow Zach to work full out on building his own ramp. I know that Andrew is interested in helping him, and if what I overhead when he was on the phone, Miss Sara Kimble has suddenly discovered an overwhelming interest in learning about skateboards."

###

Zach missed several days of school, too sore to sit for any length of time. But for the first time since they moved to Seattle, friends showed up after school to visit with him and bring his homework. Sarah was in Zach's grade; she had long blonde hair and her bright orange braces matched her T-shirt. Andrew and Angela also came each day, and Chloe made sure there were snacks available for all of them before she went back downstairs to work.

Zach was also too sore to help Deke with the construction, but he still went outside a couple times a day and sat and talked with him. Chloe couldn't hear what they were chatting about but was glad that Zach trusted Deke, because she trusted Deke to give him good advice.

Outside, Zach turned his face up to soak the meager sunlight, the first that had showed it face in a couple of days. Deke glanced at him then bent to measure his board. "How are you feeling about turning in the guys who beat you up?"

Zach sighed. "It seems wrong to rat on friends, you know?"

Deke nodded. "I know. But there are friends and then there are friends. And if your friends break the law and then beat you up, it might be time to trade them in."

He paused and then took a deep breath, "Zach, I had a prison record by the time I was your age." Zach turned a shocked face toward him. "I got caught up in the wrong crowd; I didn't have any adults who cared about who I ran with and the decisions I made. I was arrested for grand theft auto when I was fourteen." He winced inwardly at the almost admiration in the youngster's eyes and ruthlessly squashed it, "Crime is not glamorous, and the consequences will ruin your life. What you did was gutsy and right. I am proud of you."

Deke handed Zach a metal box roughly in the shape of a triangle. A ring tied to a piece of string hung out one end. "This is a plumb line. You hook this metal ring on one end of a vertical wall," he demonstrated, "and allow the box to drop. It will fall in a perfectly straight line, along which you can check to see if the wall you've erected is perfectly straight."

He paused, there was so much that could be said here, he just didn't know how preachy it would come across. "An eight-foot wall that is out of plumb one inch at the foundation will be off by twelve inches at the top. That's why cornerstones were so important in buildings in early times, before we had modern equipment. The cornerstone set the plumb line for the entire building." He took a breath and decided he had to take the chance, even if it did come across preachy, "Your values have to have a cornerstone to build on. That's why it's so important to know the Bible; it's the only true foundation on which to build your values. Once you understand what the Bible teaches, you can use it as your plumb line to make decisions and know that you're building your life correctly."

He waited, almost without breathing. Zach considered the words, and finally turned to look him in the face, "So you think that squealing on my friends is what the Bible teaches me to do?"

"First of all, I thought you said that TJ wasn't a friend; he was just another skateboarder at the park."

"Yeah," his shoulders hunched. Deke's heart went out to him; it wasn't very easy to break away from the herd and the code—such as it was—that teens went by.

"And friends don't trap other friends in illegal activities without understanding that there could be consequences."

"Yeah," Zach wasn't convinced.

"Finally, what is the higher authority here? Friends or the law? To what or whom do you owe allegiance?" Boy he was piling it on thick, but the kid needed a reality check.

"I guess it would be the law. But everybody will know I snitched," the look of panic on Zach's face made his heart clench.

He couldn't help himself, without his knowing how it happened, his arm went around Zach's shoulders, and he gave him a big hug. "Zach, doing something hard, even when you know it's the right thing to do, often has short-term, unpleasant reactions, but that is the whole point of building your life on God's Word. You can trust God, do what's right, and let the rest play out, knowing that God is pleased with you, even if nobody else is. And for what it's worth, your mom and I are proud of you."

Chapter 16

Chloe didn't have time to sit at her desk and take care of any paperwork until mid-morning. She waited until snacks had been enjoyed, and then when her two workers gathered all the kids for project time, she motioned that she was going to her desk to work. Maria nodded in understanding, beginning the opening lines to Shel Silberstein's' "Boa Constrictor, Boa Constrictor," with the kids chiming in with glee.

She was preoccupied scanning the mail that had just arrived so felt for her chair with her hip, and sat down to open the bills. As her bottom hit the chair pad, a wheel popped out of its slot, the chair tilted, and before she could shift her weight and catch herself, the seat came apart and she fell to the floor. She was aware that the noise had alerted Maria, but she couldn't catch her breath because of the pain in her leg. Sweat popped out on her forehead and for a moment everything receded in a haze around her. Her stomach revolted and she was very afraid she was going to throw up.

"Chloe?" Maria's face materialized above her, eyes wide with concern. Behind her eight preschoolers peered anxiously at her, and even in the midst of her pain, her eyes searched for and found Daniel's. He was standing with both hands clapped alongside his face, eyes huge in the wire-framed glasses, staring at her in horror.

"Daniel?" she said weakly, and fainted. She wasn't out very long. The next thing she realized, Deke was there, tucking a blanket around her shoulders, and holding his cell phone to his ear. She dimly heard him give her address and instruct Maria to take the children back to the other room. She drifted in and out of consciousness, sucking in her breath at the pain each time she roused and eagerly grabbing the grey shroud of unconsciousness back around her.

She was vaguely aware when the EMTs arrived and a needle was inserted into her arm, then blessed blankness descended.

###

In the waiting room the air was tense. Deke had been waiting outside school when Zach emerged, and he'd practically jumped out of his skin, knowing that something was wrong. "What happened?" his eyes huge holes in his face, telegramming his fear.

Deke hurried to reassure him, "Your mom fell; she's in the hospital, but she'll be fine. I thought you'd like to know as soon as possible. I'll take you right now if you'd like."

Zach hadn't hesitated, He'd wrenched open the passenger door and climbed in, hauling in his backpack and skateboard in a rush.

Deke didn't say anything on the drive; he knew Zach was hurting. He knew he was facing the possibility of losing his only remaining parent. He reached across and gripped Zach's shoulder, "She's going to be fine, son." The name just came out of nowhere, but Zach didn't seem to hear it. "She sprained her knee, broke an ankle and bruised herself, but she will be perfectly fine." Zach still didn't respond; he stared straight ahead, but the stiffness in his body began to relax.

###

When she awoke, she had the strong impression

that several hours had passed. She lay quietly, her eyes barely open, assessing her condition. Her head felt full of cotton and her mouth was dry. Turning her head in search of water, she saw Deke sitting quietly beside her in a chair.

At her movement, he stood and walked to the edge of her bed, "Hi."

"What happened?" she croaked.

"I'm afraid Daniel got into some tools again and fixed your chair."

"That little scamp; he's so out of there."

Deke smiled, "Daniel's daddy has already been to the hospital; he's called twice, and he sent those," he nodded his head toward the other side of her bed.

She gingerly turned her head to see the biggest bouquet of flowers she'd ever seen before. "Looks like a funeral bouquet, all it needs is a three-legged stand," she muttered.

Deke grinned, "To say he's upset and anxious about his little boy's future is an understatement."

She moaned, "What am I going to do with that kid? Someday it won't be me he hurts, it will be another child, and I'll be up to my armpits in a lawsuit."

Deke sighed, "I'm not sure, but I have been praying about a solution, and there may be a way to direct Daniel's inquisitiveness." Deke was quiet for a moment and then continued with his updates, "I sent Zach to the cafeteria to get some supper; he'll be back in a few moments, and it would be good for you to be awake and allay his fears that you're dying."

She swallowed, "Thanks for everything Deke. I appreciate your help today." She sighed, "I don't know what I'm going to do about Zach tonight."

He knew that if she hadn't been high on drugs she would never have admitted her worry to him. He thought he'd better tread carefully, "Chloe, I'll be glad to sleep on the couch at your apartment tonight if you don't want Zach to be alone. Or I can take him home with me and keep him at my place. Just tell me what makes you feel best."

She sighed, wishing her head didn't feel like it was filled with cotton wool. "I don't want him at home by himself until we get this drug stuff straightened out. I think he's in danger, even though he doesn't take it seriously. Please, would you please take him home with you?"

Zach entered the room at that moment, peering hesitantly around the door. She didn't blame him; he'd had enough of hospitals, as had she, in the last months of Phillip's life. She turned her head and smiled at him reassuringly, "Daniel strikes again, Zach. This time he scored."

The relief in his face made tears well up in her eyes and that made his eyes opened even wider. Thankfully, Deke intervened. "Way to go, Zach. Show any mom sympathy, and they're guaranteed to cry."

Zach grinned a wobbly grin, and Chloe said, "Deke suggested you sleep at his house tonight."

That ruined the mood, immediately Zach's face screwed up, and he opened his mouth to protest, but something in her face and Deke's demeanor made him rethink his reaction and he muttered, "Okay, Mom, if that makes you feel better." He shifted uneasily on his feet, and Deke stood up.

"Guess we'd better head home and let your mom

get some sleep." His hand covered her foot and the heat soothed her, "Rest Chloe. I'll stop by after everyone gets to work and Zach gets to school and see what the doc says about releasing you."

She gazed at him out of drugged eyes, but she knew the fabric of him. She knew the integrity of him, his kindness to Daniel, his gentle friendship with her son, and she knew he was someone she could trust. She closed her eyes and sighed, "Night son. Be sure and feed Maleficent before you go." As she drifted back under the grey cloud hovering above her head, she realized that she was comforted knowing he was going to be with Deke.

###

As Deke might have suspected, Zach balked the minute they were in the hallway. "I can stay at home by myself," the stubborn jut of his chin told Deke he might have quite a fight on his hands.

"I know, I know," Deke held up his hands in surrender, "but it's your mom we need to be thinking of right now. She's hurt, and, because she's mom, she's worried about you. We can't do anything about her pain, but we can alleviate her worry, so how 'bout it? Come stay the night at my place. I'm sure she'll be released tomorrow." Zach sighed and Deke took it as capitulation.

It was almost an hour before Deke pushed the nose of his pickup up his driveway. They had dropped by the apartment for Zach to pack a change of clothing. He had been surprisingly responsible, making sure that all the doors and windows were locked and Maleficent was fed before gathering clothes and jamming them into his backpack.

Deke pulled the truck to a halt in front of his house. They walked in, and he stood inside the door watching Zach examine his home. The first thing Zach noticed were the books. They lined three of his four walls, stacked into floor-to-ceiling bookcases, they wrapped the doorways, climbed the walls, turned the corner out of site, as if they marched down the hall. It was obvious to any observer that he was a book lover. They were not collector copies, the majority of them were paperbacks and their colorful spines gave the room a cheery hominess. “Wow, Mom would love this room,” he exclaimed, and Deke felt a glow of satisfaction.

Three-quarters of the home, all of it visible from the front door, was a great room. The kitchen was across from the front door, along the backside of the house. A butcher-block island stood in front of the sink. From the front door, Zach could see a glass-topped door that opened out to the backyard. The kitchen table was made of warm oak and something about its craftsmanship made Zach wonder if Deke had made it himself. A big corduroy covered couch and two chairs were arranged in a semi-circle around a rock fireplace that abutted the end wall of the great room. On a rug in front of it lay big Woofer, who uncurled himself at their entrance and quietly padded to sit before them.

“Hey, Woofer,” Zach reached out and scratched his ears. He was obviously glad to connect to something familiar.

A quiet undercurrent of noise pulled Zach’s eyes to a ledge fixed approximately a foot from the ceiling. A miniature railroad track circled the room, and an engine pulling eight cars slowly made its way around the circumference. Every few seconds, small spurts of smoke rose from the stack, and once or twice a quiet “whoo-whooo” of a whistle sounded. Set along intervals over the track, Zach could see tiny towns and stations it passed and an occasional water tank set against the wall. “Wow,” he breathed, looking around, “Cool.”

Deke grinned at his wide-eyed reaction. "It's a vintage Lionel from the 1930s. I bought it on eBay five years ago. It was in pretty bad shape but it ran, and that was what was important for me, since I'm no electrician. Took me over a year to restore and repaint it. It's my concession to my missing childhood." He punched a switch on the wall that he had automatically flipped on with the lights when they entered, and the train slowly came to a halt. He walked over, stretched to unhook the engine, and handed it to Zach. "It's made of tinplate metal; you can buy factory restoration paints, and that's what I used."

Zach reverently cradled it in his hands, admiring the glossy finish and detailing. "I never had a train. Dad and I had race cars, but I never even thought about wanting a train," his head came up, "but I do now. I'm telling Mom I want one for Christmas." Deke laughed.

Stairs along the back wall of the great room led to a second floor. He showed Zach a daybed in one of the bedrooms and the shower next door then left him to settle in. The teen joined him a few minutes later, seeming ill at ease, wandering around the room taking everything in.

"How about if you call your grandma? I'm sure she will want to know what happened."

Zach nodded, "I already texted my cousin, Ryan, from the hospital, but I guess I should talk to Grandma." He put his cell to his ear and walked into the great room.

In a moment, Zach approached him, holding out his cell, "Grandma wants to speak to you," rolling his eyes, "she wants to make sure you're not an axe murderer or something."

Deke held the phone to his ear. "This is Deke Hudson."

A light and feminine voice floated into his ear. "Deke, thank you so much for helping out Chloe and Zach. You are God's angel of mercy today. Tell me, how is Chloe, really? I've only had sketchy details at best."

He told her what the doctor had said to Chloe while he was in the room. "I imagine she'll be released tomorrow, but I don't think she'll be able to return to work for a while. She won't have had time to decide what to do with her business."

"Oh, that won't be a problem," the warm voice assured him. "Her sister and I are already packing. We'll be there tomorrow afternoon and will take over the day care until she is well enough to run it again."

He felt awkward being privy to Chloe's private affairs without her permission. He hoped that her mother knew what she was doing making this decision for Chloe. The boss he knew would not appreciate anyone making decisions for her, but maybe a mother was different. What did he know? "Well, I'm sure that will be a big help to her," he said diplomatically.

He punched the Off button and handed Zach his phone as he walked back to the kitchen. Zach had eaten a hamburger at the hospital, but it wasn't enough to fuel a teen. Besides Deke was hungry himself. Before he could do more than open the fridge door, his back door swung open, and Mrs. Watanabe entered. The smell of hot rice and beef filled the air and brought Zach to the kitchen doorway. His eyes widened at the sight of the tiny figure, holding a three-level rice steamer almost as tall as herself.

Deke introduced him, "Mrs. Watanabe, meet Zach Evans. He's staying with me tonight while his mom's in the hospital."

He was inordinately pleased to see Zach step forward and take the steamer out of the older woman's hands and place it on the counter. He rubbed his palms on his jeans and stuck out his hand to shake hers, asking eagerly, "Pleased to meet you. Is that food for us?"

"I knew that hospital food, even if you could get it down, wouldn't be enough to help you two sleep tonight," she said, unloading the bamboo tiers and filling two plates that Deke placed on the counter. There was fluffy rice in the top tier. The one below held fragrant strips of beef that lay with plump mushrooms, sliced water chestnuts, bamboo shoots, and green onions in a dark sauce.

"Sit, sit," she instructed and placed filled plates before each of them.

Zach and Deke dug in like they were starving, and she watched them eat in satisfaction. Within a few minutes, the plates were empty, and she restacked her warmer to leave.

"I'll just walk her home," Deke said to Zach and followed her out the door. Woofer looked back and forth in indecision but in the end elected to remain with Zach. When he returned a few minutes later, Zach was back in the great room watching the train make its rotation, his hand rubbing Woofer's head.

He turned when Deke entered, "Wow, she's even smaller than Mom. Although," he added perceptively, "I bet she can be just as tough as Mom."

Deke grinned, "Yes, they're two of a kind. They'll either be great friends or ardent enemies." Zach didn't appear to find it unusual that Deke thought they'd be meeting some time.

Instead, he reached to the top of his Mohawk and ruffled the edges with his hand, "Hey, Deke? Do you think you could shave my head for me?"

"Get rid of your Mohawk?" Deke gasped in mock

horror. "Maybe your mom doesn't want it gone."

"Yeah, I'm sure she'll be disappointed. She practically bites her tongue in half every time she looks at me."

"I don't know, man, if you shave it you'll be left with a blue skunk stripe down the back of your head. Would that be any better?"

Zach rolled his eyes at the stupidity of adults, "The color's washable. It'll come right out. Are you going to do it or what?"

"Oh, I'm going to do it, right now before you change your mind."

Twenty minutes later, Deke stood behind Zach, looking over the top of his head as Zach stared at his newly-shorn self in the mirror. Before shaving, he'd removed all his jewelry except for one stud in his ear. With the Mohawk gone the strong bones in his face were revealed. He was going to be a very handsome man. He must look like his dad because it was only in his expressions that Deke could see Chloe.

"What do you think?"

Zach grinned, "I look like my normal dweeb self. I think I'm glad to be back to normal."

Deke slapped him on the shoulder. Well, you will make your mom a happy woman when she sees you tomorrow. Let's hit the hay; we've got to get up early."

Zach paused on the bottom step, "Do you mind getting me up in time for school? Unless," he eyed him hopefully, "do you think Mom would mind if I miss classes tomorrow? I probably ought to stay home and help around the day care."

"Nice try, champ," Deke raised an eyebrow. "But

you and I both know that your mom would want you at school as usual."

Zach sighed in defeat, "Yeah, you're right. Okay, get me up in time to go by the house and feed Maleficent. She'll tear the house apart if we've left her without any food."

"You got it. Breakfast at six-thirty, then we'll swing by your house, and I'll drive you to school afterwards so you won't be late."

"Cool," his head disappeared and Deke turned out the lights and went to bed himself.

As he lay in bed, he reviewed the events of the day. He was so glad he had been around when Chloe had her accident; it had hurt him seeing her in such pain, but he knew that she was easier in her mind knowing he would keep an eye on Zach. Watching the transformation in Zach tonight opened something in his heart. He knew that God had forgiven him for his part in the abortion many years ago. But Chloe's words came back, and he acknowledged that he had never forgiven himself.

Now, looking at a possibility of a future with Chloe and himself, he could accept that he needed to release himself from his old guilt. It was much too heavy for him to carry any longer. That was precisely why Christ had died – to give anyone who accepted it, freedom from guilt. He was ready to accept the future and what God had planned for him, whether or not it included Chloe and Zach, he was going to walk in freedom from now on.

Chapter 17

Chloe's night was uncomfortable. Between fitful bouts of sleep, aching all over, and the nurses bustling in every hour to check her pupils, she was glad to see dawn creeping around the edges of her blinds. At seven a.m., her bedside phone rang, and she picked up the receiver attached to the bed rail, wincing as pain radiated down her spine. "Hello?"

"Darling!" Faith's light-as-air-voice floated out into the room. "Zach and I spoke last night, and he told me all about your fall. I am so sorry you're laid up. But don't worry! Maddie and I will come and help you out for a couple of weeks."

She couldn't hold back a groan. This was all she needed—to be laid up and have her mom for company. "Mom, don't worry about me and Zach. He's old enough to help me at home, and I have dependable workers at the day care. You don't need to come." She might as well be batting at shadows.

"Honey, it's okay. That's what family is for. We're delighted to help out. Good thing I kept my day care license current; I'll be able to step in and take over until you're good as new." Chloe hung up in defeat, she just hoped that when her mom left she would still have a day care to run.

Breakfast was inedible. Even the coffee was horrid. What she wouldn't give for a cup of Starbucks or Seattle's Best. Midmorning, they let her up to take a shower, but she had to don her old clothes as nobody had thought to bring her fresh clothing. Every time footsteps passed close to her door she looked up eagerly, expecting the doctor to come in and release her to go home. Her wait was interrupted at eleven a.m. for an even more unremarkable lunch, and finally at one-thirty, the doctor swept into the room. He poked and prodded her, explained she had a concussion and what to watch for in recovery, shared the x-rays that said she had indeed fractured her left ankle. He explained that the swelling on her knee would reduce in a couple of days, but until then she was to wear the inflatable cast that encased her leg and have bed rest. She was to call and make an appointment to see him at the end of week, and if everything looked okay, he would probably release her for part-time work. He then asked who would be home to help her and seemed satisfied with her response, because he signed her release.

She endured another hour before Deke and Zach arrived just after three. She was so glad to see them she could have hugged them both, but Zach was a surprise. "Honey, you shaved!" She hoped the lilt in her voice wouldn't set him off in a snit.

He grinned, almost shame-faced, "Yeah, decided I was done with being cool. Besides it took a lot of time to keep it standing straight and the color on. I've got other stuff to do and don't have time to take care of it. Deke shaved my head last night for me."

She didn't care why he'd done it; she was just incredibly happy that he had. She knew intuitively that Zach had turned some corner within himself and no longer needed his outward armor anymore. She looked at Deke with gratitude, and he smiled back at her.

"Whoa," Deke grabbed her arm as she stood up, which turned out to be a good thing as the room immediately tilted and whirled. Their voices receded, and she concentrated on not throwing up. When it settled, Zach was holding her other arm and both of them were watching her in consternation.

"Well, guess I won't try that again soon," she smiled, not willing to scare her son anymore than he already was.

"Right," Deke eyed her warily, "why don't you sit back down on the edge of the bed," he helped her perch then reached around her to press the call button, "and we'll wait for the nurse to come and help you leave the building."

Her nurse entered, along with the hospital escort pushing a wheelchair. "All set to go?" she said brightly. She maneuvered the chair at a ninety-degree angle to the bed. Reaching she took Chloe's arm and helped her to slowly stand and then turn and sit in the wheelchair. With Deke holding doors for them and Zach carrying her stuff, she was paraded down the hallway, to the elevator, and out to the hospital lobby. Deke had parked the Cherokee in the pick-up zone, and he rolled her to the passenger side. Again, she gingerly stood and awkwardly attempted to climb into the cab. Finally she gave up and stared mutinously at the seat, perched too high for her to slide into.

Deke didn't say anything, he simply stooped and gathered her in his arms and set her onto the seat. He reached across and fastened her seatbelt for her. Zach tumbled into the back. After stowing her belongings into the back and handing Zach two flower arrangements, they were off.

"What is the damage?" Deke turned his head to smile at her. She couldn't believe how happy she was to be out of the hospital. You would have thought she'd been incarcerated half a lifetime. Her head eagerly scanned the sidewalk, the sunshine showing a happy scene outside the cab.

"I have a concussion and a fractured left leg." Deke whistled in dismay. "I have to remain on bed rest until I go to see the doctor sometime later this week—I have to call for an appointment when I get home. Once I can use a walking cast, he'll release me for light work duty."

He turned to Chloe and hesitated, "I've been thinking about Daniel."

She groaned, "As much as I love him, it's too dangerous to have him around. What if that had happened to one of the children? I don't care whether or not I was sued; nothing would ever allow me to forgive myself."

He nodded, understanding her dilemma, "Would you consider keeping him if I helped you come up with a solution for his adventurous interest? I wonder if it would help if we promised Daniel a special treat if he does exactly what you tell him to all day?"

She didn't allow herself to pause on his "we" but responded, "What are you thinking?"

"I could let him come out with me for fifteen minutes at the end of each day he behaves and work with my tools." He assured her, "I'll be with him every minute and watch him carefully. I assure you he will not get hurt."

She mulled it over aloud, "Offering a special treat to one child—in effect a bribe—doesn't sit well with me. But on the other hand, he is usually the last child here each day so the others might not necessarily find out about it, although…"

"…on the third hand?" Deke grinned watching her wrestle with the temptation of bringing Daniel under control by rewarding bad behavior with a special treat.

"Well, I was a rule follower myself, and I know how enraging it was to watch special enticements given to miscreants to help them behave, while not giving treats to those who already towed the line." Her eyes flashed just at the memory.

"Well, then add Tool Time to your class schedule, and rotate all of them through it."

"No," she frowned at him, "I want my remodel done this fall, not next summer." She nodded her head decisively, "No, there won't be a Tool Time, but yes, I will accept your offer for Daniel. And we will find something just as special for all the others who will miss it." She nodded, obviously pleased with her decision.

Once again, he was struck by the difference between her business persona and her mother mode. She was straight-forward and in control as Business Chloe, but she folded like a cheap billfold as Mother Chloe. Too bad she didn't allow the Business Chloe to flow over into the Mother Chloe. No doubt Zach's attitude would have improved much earlier if she had.

"Thank you," her eyes met his; she appreciated him realizing the gravity of this particular four-year-old's potential.

Chapter 18

Chloe knew to the second when Faith McKinnon Dyer walked in her front door. Even one floor up, she felt the atmospheric change in the entire building. Faith altered any environment she entered. She heard Zach shout, "Grandma! Auntie Maddie!" And moments later the door to the apartment slammed back on its hinges. Help had arrived.

"Sweetie," Faith swooped to the bedside and enveloped her in a mist of White Shoulders, her signature scent since 1964. Just like that, Chloe was transported to grade school when she had occasionally been home with the flu and her mom's hug and presence had been the best medicine. "How are you feeling? That little Daniel opened the door for us at the bottom of the stairs. You really should keep the door locked you know, one of them could wander away without the help realizing it."

Chloe attempted an answer, "We usually do, we just thought that I may need help and wouldn't be able to get up to unlock it if so."

"Of course, so logical as always."

She eyed her mom's attire. Faith's usual style was retro-country. Today she was wearing a long light corduroy dress in pale aqua that buttoned with little silver discs down the front. A brown leather belt circled her still trim waist and was decorated with turquoise and silver studs. Below the hem peeked worn brown cowboy boots with silver toes. As usual, she looked both chic and comfortable. Around her neck, her eyeglasses swung on a chain made of dyed penne pasta, no doubt created by one of her adoring preschool friends, of whom she had many. Her still blonde hair was gathered at the back of her neck in a braided coil.

Chloe's sister entered the room, toting three bags. Naturally Faith hadn't thought that the bags needed to make it from the car into the house, or maybe she assumed they would do it on their own. Maddie dropped two bags with a thump in the middle of the floor and unhooked the duffel slung over her shoulder. She followed her mom to the bed to hug Chloe. "Hi, babe," she stood back and scrutinized her sister. "You look pretty good, but obviously aren't moving very well yet, huh?"

Zach brought up the rear, toting even more suitcases. He slid the strap of a bag off his shoulder, his face bright with excitement at his grandmother and aunt's arrival, "I wish Ryan could have come."

Faith hugged Zach, "Darling boy, you are such a help. I'd give you a tip but I'm broke."

Maddie grinned, "Used all her cash to buy lunches at McDonald for the homeless and," her grin got bigger, "one businessman she said was grumpy and needed a lift." Chloe laughed in spite of herself. No one did irrepressible like their mom.

Something about Zach's stance caught her attention. She eyed him closely. He was cradling something in his arms, and her sense of foreboding grew as he neared. He had a dog. At least she thought it was a dog. Tiny, hairless, and if she was the type to jump to conclusions, she'd have thought it was a rat.

"Look!" Zach loosened his arms to reveal a shivering bag of bones. The lollipop head on its stick neck peered at her as if it sensed the danger of immediate banishment from the kingdom. "It's a Chihuahua," he added unnecessarily and scooped it closed again. The critter tucked its nose in Zach's armpit, turning his head away from the enemy. "Grandma found it at McDonald's. And since it didn't have a tag and the workers said it had been hanging around for days, she didn't want to leave it to get run over. So she brought it to me."

"How kind," Chloe muttered ironically.

Maddie grinned in sympathy, "She discovered him when she emptied her purse buying Happy Meals," she waggled her eyebrows, inviting Chloe to share her amusement. Chloe felt the dual bubble of laughter and tightness in her head she always experienced in the vicinity of her mom.

Chloe wasn't surprised to see Deke appear holding three more suitcases. She had known that one trip apiece for Maddie and Zach would not empty the car, especially since Faith wouldn't be doing any emptying herself. Faith could be on a deserted island and males would come out of nowhere to help her. Her air of fragility got them every time. Maddie and she had the same fragile appearance, but they didn't trade on it like Mom. It might have something to do with her being from a different generation, Chloe wasn't sure.

Her mom looked at her perplexed, "About the dog, that's okay isn't it? If not, we can take it home when we leave."

Zach's protest rang out just as she'd known it would, "Oh, Mom, let's keep him, can't we?"

She eyed the creature shivering in Zach's arms. If there was anything she hated, it was little, nervous, yapping dogs. Her eyes went from the woebegone creature huddled in his arms, already sensing his safe harbor was not safe, to Zach's pleading eyes and sighed, "Yes, if you'll take care of him. Please tell me," her eyes cut toward her mother, "that he's housebroken."

"Well, we ought to find out pretty soon," was her mom's cheerful response, and Chloe sank back on her pillows and closed her eyes.

###

She had resigned herself to spending her days recuperating in bed. Even knowing it was for only a week did not make the isolation loom any less grimly. She was used to being active, and knowing she was going to be immobile was borderline depressing. Faith had spent the night in a guestroom, while Maddie had insisted on sharing Chloe's bed.

"You might need help getting to the potty in the night."

For her part, Chloe was glad to have her sis sleeping with her. It reminded her of how, when growing up, one of them had invariably sneaked out of her room each night to climb into the other's bed. They had chatted awhile, but drugs and exhaustion from her injuries soon had Chloe dropping off to sleep.

Maddie was up early to open the day care with Mom, sign in children, and explain the change in personnel for the foreseeable future.

Chloe remembered Zach rousing her early and clumsily to eat a bowl of cereal and a piece of fruit. She dozed until seven-thirty when she heard the buzzer for the apartment sound. A moment later she heard Zach open the door to the apartment, and then he appeared in the doorway of her bedroom to ask, "Deke's at the door and wants to know if you're ready to move to the couch?"

"Tell him," she began, but stopped when Deke's head appeared over the top of Zach's in the doorway.

He smiled, "You can't move on your own yet, but

knowing you, you'll go stark raving mad stuck in bed all day. How about if I move you to the couch for today, and we'll see if you're strong enough to go downstairs tomorrow and survey your kingdom from one of the couches there?"

She felt stupid tears gather at his perceptive realization that she would feel cut off from everything going on. She swallowed hard and smiled, "That would be great."

He stepped to the bedside and eyed her sleep attire. They were little yellow ducks on a blue background, and Zach had given them to her for Christmas when he was ten. "Love the jammies," he grinned. "Put your arms around my neck," he stooped and curled one arm around her waist and then slid the other arm under her knees to lift hcr. "Zach, take the pillows and get a blanket for your mom and put them on the couch."

Zach hurried to do his bidding, and Deke waited, not even strained, she noted, while a makeshift nest was created for her on the front room couch. He gently laid her amid the blankets, with her back propped on the end of the couch.

"Okay," he surveyed her surroundings for a moment, "cell phone?" Zach slapped it into his hand. "Water?" Zach dashed off to the kitchen while Deke moved the end table to position it within easy reach. He adjusted the floor lamp to a better position for lighting. He went back into the bedroom returning with the book she was currently reading, along with her reading glasses, and pain medication. Zach returned at the same moment with a glass of water, overfull and slopping gently, but he looked so serious she didn't have the heart to point it out.

"Has she had breakfast?" he addressed Zach.

"Yes sir," Zach stood straighter, looking dependable, "I took her a bowl of cereal and a banana at six." He grinned, "Grandma told me to."

"Good man," Zach visibly swelled under his praise. He hadn't responded with so much pride when she'd thanked him profusely earlier for his help.

"Thank you." She hated asking for help, and, from the grin on Deke's face, he knew it. "This is just so inconvenient," she fretted. "I'm messing up everyone's life."

"I don't think your accident has that much power in the scheme of the universe," Deke sounded unsympathetic. "There are a lot of people who like you," he arranged his expression to appear teasingly mystified, "and it won't hurt you to allow them to help you for once." He took one last look at the arrangements they had made for her. "Okay, guess you're on your own until lunch." He picked up her phone again, punched in a number, and handed it back. "That's my cell; I'll be around all morning so if you need anything—anything at all," he stared at her pointedly, "call me."

She reached into the pocket of her pajama jacket and pulled out a baby monitor. "I've already been given this by my mom," she said loftily. "I'm wired for anything."

He paused for a moment to observe her swathed in a kelly green afghan. The bright color of the throw drew out the copper in her hair and made her alabaster skin shine. "Beautiful blanket," he commented, enjoying the scenery.

She glanced down at it, "Thanks," she picked up a corner of the wool and ran its silkiness through her fingers. "My cousin, Miranda, is a world-class knitter. She made it for me when Zach was born. I love its softness. She's the one who's married to a preacher. She has a specialty knitting business on the internet."

He shook his head, "Just how big is your family?"

She grinned, "We're not a huge clan; we're just close."

Seeing his mystification she explained, "It's because all the cousins are girls. And we're all within a ten-year range of each other. It was a gap for some of us growing up, but now that we're adults, it's no gap at all."

He shook his head again, shelving the family, and he and Zach headed for the door.

"Bye Mom, see you after school," Zach called. "Oh, I fed Carmine, and he's around here somewhere, so watch out for him, okay?"

"Carmen, huh? Silly name for a boy dog," she heard Deke comment as they went down the stairs. She couldn't hear Zach's explanation.

Just like that, they were gone. And she was alone.

###

Maleficent slunk in from whatever hiding place she was currently using and eyed her for a moment. She started to apologize for taking her favorite sunny spot but caught herself in time. A few minutes passed and then the click of tiny toenails made both of them turn expectantly toward the kitchen. A tiny nose topped by bulgy eyes peered at them hesitantly. He immediately pulled back when spotting the cat but reappeared a moment later.

She sighed, "Come here," gently snapping her fingers. The meager remainder of the animal curled around the door and stood trembling. She made a kissing sound with her mouth and coaxed it, one inch at a time, to her side. "Well, here goes nothing," she said, scooping it up and laying it on her breast within scratching distance of Maleficent. She watched while the cat eyed the intruder from the back of the couch and the intruder tried to melt into her pajama pocket. "Well, it's evident that both of you have had at least passing acquaintance with others of your breed." She turned to Maleficent, "Thank you for not destroying this chap. Zach will be pleased." Maleficent turned her golden eyes to her and yawned mightily then looked away ignoring both of them.

Emboldened by the sense that danger had passed, the Chihuahua gingerly stretched out on her chest, minimally reduced its shivers, and fell asleep. Before she knew it, Chloe had joined both of them, and they passed the morning napping and looking out the window into the front yard.

Chapter 19

She was surprised how much her accident had affected her, but the day passed quickly due to the irritating habit of her body sinking into a nap every hour or so. At noon, Deke appeared carrying her lunch on a tray with his lunchbox tucked under his arm.

He sank into the easy chair at a right angle to her couch. He unwrapped a huge ham-cheese-and-who-knew-what-else sandwich and took a big bite. He chewed appreciatively, swallowed, and turned to her.

"I like your family. Your mom is a kick, and Maddie is real nice. How many kids are there in your family?"

"Just us two girls. Like I said, girls run in the McKinnon family. Uncle Robert has four daughters, Uncle Ralph has two girls, and Mom has us two."

"But you and Maddie broke the mold with sons?"

"Yup, I had one son, no girls, and Maddie has one son and two girls."

"I actually envy you your family," he admitted, stretching out long legs beside her.

"My family?" she turned her head to stare at him. He stared straight ahead, a smile edging his mouth, while she added incredulously, "Have you spent any time with my mother?"

"She really bugs you doesn't she?" he said softly. "She's iconoclastic."

"She's a fifty-seven-year-old woman who still believes she's twenty-five and invincible," she sputtered.

"Actually, she is pretty close to invincible." He shifted to stare at her. "What bugs you the most about her? Her clothes? Her bleeding heart? What? Do you know what I would have given growing up to have a mother who drops everything to come when I needed help?"

Guilt needled her, "I know I'm an ungrateful louse, and I do love her, but," she swooped both hands through her hair and thrust them upwards, "what's wrong with conforming, just a little bit? She was the only mother wearing a hat to my eighth grade mother-daughter tea, and it didn't have roses on it. Oh no, it had a broody hen on top with baby chicks peeking out from underneath around the sides." He snorted, suppressing a chuckle, and she continued, "She still goes TP-ing with the youth group on Friday nights." The snort turned into a bellow of laughter.

"All my life, whenever someone recognizes me, the first thing they say is, 'I remember when your mother…'" Her shoulders drooped, "I know I'm an adult; I know I should have come to a resolution, and when she's not around, I do. I have. But then she shows up with a stray dog she's picked up on the way, and I forget all my good intentions and get angry all over again."

Chloe shrugged and gave a deprecating grin, "Maybe I'm jealous because she always leads with her heart and somehow it always works out. I remember one time she gave away all of the toys from the church's day care because she'd heard the Boys and Girls Club was starting a day care and needed donations. And the very next day, the Presbyterians called and said they were closing down their day care and asked if she wanted their toys for hers? It's like she has special dispensation to never reap what she sows!"

"Oh, she always reaps what she sows," Deke grinned. "It sounds like she sows butterflies and love and reaps a harvest just as sweet."

After a moment he turned his head to gaze over her head out the window. "At least she cares. My story isn't so American Pie. My mom cared too—about her latest boyfriend, her booze, and having a good time. She cared about a lot of things, but none of them were her son."

She gazed at him aghast. "Deke," she breathed. "I, I don't know what to say." She was horrified. Especially seeing what a good upstanding man he was. She couldn't believe that he had survived such a childhood.

She tilted her head, "Something had to happen in order for you to turn out to be such a great person."

He turned his head and she could see him sorting his memories as he met her gaze, "A patrol officer happened. David Menodine was passionate about helping teens. I was fourteen when I was arrested for stealing, and David was the officer who caught me. Somehow, he saw something worth salvaging. After I was released from juvie, he became my mentor while I completed probation, and when I finished he petitioned the court to be my foster parent. I moved in with him, his wife, and their two kids. He was tough, fair, and the very best thing that ever happened to me.

"He not only taught me how a man should act, but the importance of working hard and keeping my word. They showed me how to be a big brother to their boys, and Bea fed me every time I turned around. They bought me shoes that fit, and she kept my clothes clean and mended. They took me to church and got me involved in their church's youth group. Before I knew it, I had goals and a new life."

He smiled tenderly, "And Bea taught me about Jesus. Dave was a believer too, but found it hard to talk about his faith, but Bea, she just breathed her relationship with God and it made sense, you know?"

"Yeah, I do know. I just wish I had my mom's faith."

"However, while it made sense, I didn't become born again until I joined the Army and was in Afghanistan. War certainly brings what's important to the surface, and I suddenly realized that believing in God and having a relationship with God were two different things. I suddenly wasn't satisfied with believing in Him, I wanted to know Him."

He stared off at a dark scene in his mind, "For all their goodness and help, Dave and Bea just weren't aware of how much darkness there was inside me. They didn't know about the baby until my girlfriend and I had already aborted it. I'd never seen Bea cry, and it fairly killed me that I was the reason she was so heartbroken."

He glanced at her face and then wished he hadn't. The naked pain in her eyes shook him and he was aware of how vulnerable he was to her. After a moment, she cleared her throat then attempted a smile, "Everyone has moments and events in their lives which we wish we could do over. Even Dave and Bea will have had them, if you only knew. It's not the mistakes that we make that define us, it's what we learn and do after committing them that makes us who we become. And you have become a strong, empathetic man. I know they are very proud of you."

They finished their lunch in contemplative silence, and then Deke took the dishes and headed back downstairs and out to work.

Throughout the day, the workers all found their way upstairs to commiserate with her injuries and to assure her that her mom and Maddie were handling the classes wonderfully. She really hadn't thought it would be any other way. She knew her mother had passed on her giftedness with children to both her and Maddie, and the kids were in good hands.

Tasha and Zach came tromping up the stairs together after school, laughing and shoving each other in their eagerness to be the first one into the room. Tasha was Valley girl today. A short pleated skirt in red and black plaid, white blouse with a lacy collar, and a black cardigan. Her hair was in two French braids, tied with perky red bows.

As soon as he entered the room, Zach scooped up Carmine and stuck him in his oversized pants' pocket. He introduced the dog to Tasha who protested, "Carmen's a girl's name, that's a male dog."

"Nuh-uh," Zach replied. "Not Carmen, Carmine. Like Carmine Ragusa from Laverne & Shirley." Chloe grinned to herself. She had to tell Maddie that their love of classic sitcoms had passed on to another generation.

Eyeing the pooch in Zach pocket, it was obvious from Carmine's knobby head and bulging eyes in avid observation that he liked his front-row seat.

A moment later, Woofer, bounded in, his tail banging the door back on its hinges. Immediately, Carmine dove into the bottom of Zach's pocket. Noticing the fabric trembling with his shivers, Woofer eagerly investigated, snuffling at the bulge, but he quickly lost interest and flopped down in the middle of the floor.

Daring that danger had passed, the Chihuahua's little head poked back out, and he squeaked an outraged protest. Zach reached down and rubbed his little head,

"Finally found your voice, huh boy? That big old bully is all gone, you're safe." Carmine yipped again and allowed Tasha to coo and pet him.

###

The next day Chloe ran a fever, and despite her protests neither her mom nor Deke would allow her to venture downstairs. She was mad and had meant to pout but instead she napped most of the day.

The third day she felt marginally better, so Maddie helped her shower, sitting on a plastic chair from the day care that Maddie set in the tub. Chloe felt much better with clean hair again. She also dressed fully for the first time since her accident and waited impatiently for Deke to arrive and help her downstairs

When he appeared in her doorway, he was a few minutes early. "I need to avoid Daniel," he said, gathering Chloe up and marching down the stairs. "I got an emergency phone call from a friend who owns a construction business, and he needs me to help him put a roof on a home in Everett before the expected rains get inside and do any damage. So I'm going to run out there today, and someone needs to explain to Daniel why he won't get any tool time today."

They had set up a tool time for Daniel like Deke had suggested. And just as Deke had expected, he had been an angel. He stayed with the group and hadn't even dismantled anything, although that may have been due to having already torn apart anything accessible in his short time at The Perfect Child.

After the second tool time, he had shown up at preschool wearing a little plastic tool belt. Deke gave Daniel's dad points for noticing his son's fascination with building. Now, Daniel spent every spare moment in the day tightening screws on furniture. As Chloe said, "At least he's not loosening them; he's tightening them, so we should be fine." Deke thought it was more likely that the toddler's motor skills were not defined enough for him to move the wrench counter-clockwise since he was left-handed.

For two days now, at four forty-five, a time when the majority of the kids had gone home and those who hadn't were engrossed in a special Tasha activity that she and Chloe had concocted for just this reason, Daniel was escorted outside to work with Deke's tools for fifteen blissful minutes. Deke couldn't believe what a kick he got out of helping Daniel hammer nails, measure wood, and find nails with his stud finder. Encircling the sturdy form with his arms, he more than once had to close his eyes as long-buried emotions rose up at the thought of a small son of his own to teach and enjoy. Each time he stamped it out, refusing to return to painful memories from long ago.

She offered no sympathy though, "Coward."

"I know. I know." He deposited her in the play room then stood upright and rubbed his neck defensively, "It's just that he's such a enthusiastic little guy, disappointing him is like kicking a kitten. I just can't do it."

"And you accuse me of being a softy with kids."

"Well, you are," he huffed in defeat, "and I guess I am too."

The day was fun; she read and put puzzles together with any of the children who came to visit. She realized how much she had missed them as they cuddled in her arms. She refused to stare sadly out the window.

Maddie grinned once when she caught her staring, "Miss him? He'll be back tomorrow, he promised."

Zach carefully helped her hop up the steps on her good foot when he arrived after school. In exhaustion she dropped onto the sofa and promptly fell asleep. She didn't arouse until Mom brought her supper on a plate, and they all gathered in the living room to watch Jeopardy.

"Great," Zach enthused. "We never get to eat in front of the TV. Mom, I hope your foot heals slowly."

She returned his grin, "Enjoy it, son, it's only until I get two good feet under me again."

Deke dropped by after supper to check on her and she severely quelled the thrill, seeing him in the doorway. "How are you feeling?" He set a bright pink azalea on the end table by her head. "It reminded me of you, bright and energetic, so I bought it."

She regretted the surge of color in her cheeks and the fact that her mom and Maddie immediately remembered that the dishes were waiting to be done, disappearing as soon as they let him into the room. To cover her confusion, she gestured, "Please, sit down. Thank you for the plant. It's gorgeous."

He sat in the big easy chair and stretched out his long legs on the hassock. "How did my buddy Daniel do today without his tool time?"

"Well, Daniel was very miffed that his friend Deke did not come to work. He told Mom he could work outside by himself because you said he could."

Deke grinned, "He did, huh? Any chance he got away with it?"

"Not any at all."

"Poor, Daniel. I bet I'm in the doghouse."

"Yes you are, and not just with Daniel. Zach was pretty bummed that you weren't here either. I have a feeling I'm going to have to hire you for remodeling projects for the rest of my life in order to appease my boys."

He chuckled, "Well, I could give you a cut-rate I guess." He paused, "Have you ever considered expanding your business?"

"No, I'd need a whole new facility to add more children. I not only don't have the money, I don't want to leave my home; I like it here."

"I wasn't talking about this building. I was thinking about the second floor over your garage. It would make a perfect place for afterschool care for older kids."

She was interested; he could see it in the tilt of her head. "I'd never considered something like that. I have families that sometimes leave because I don't have facilities for their older children. They like the convenience of the kids being in once place for ease in picking up and dropping off. Hmm, I never thought about it. I wouldn't need much in special furnishings, just up-to-code bathrooms and a kitchen and window bars and..." she trailed off.

"I went online a few days ago when it occurred to me and printed off the requirements for afterschool care, grades three to six. I've highlighted all the stuff that you would need to do." He handed her a printout sheaf of papers.

She ruffled through several pages, dismayed at the amount of yellow highlighting she saw. "There's a lot more than I expected," she admitted.

"Yes, but most of it is actually cosmetic and not very expensive. You have to have new stairs, bathrooms, kitchen, and floor covering, but the rest of it is elbow-grease stuff, which Zach could be roped into helping.

Plus, I bet if you asked for a workday, your whole family would come down and help. I will too. The margin between surviving in a business and actually making a profit is small, but I think with this, you could see revenue that would put you in the black in a big way."

She stared at the pages. She didn't know what to say. In just a little over a month's time, Deke had become such a friend to her and her son. She hated that he occupied so much of her thoughts. He had never given her any indication that he thought of her as more than a friend, and she wondered why, if she wasn't interested in a relationship, that bothered her so much.

"Do you mind if I keep this for a few days and do some calculating on my own?"

"Of course not, they're yours. If you need any help with estimates, give me a call; I'll be glad to give you my guess for cost and labor."

He sat back then and looked at her closely, "Enough about that, how are you feeling?"

"Like a caged animal," she admitted. "Do you realize that I haven't left this house once since the accident?"

He nodded consolingly, "Three days. I can imagine you're going crazy."

She was on a roll, "Zach has walked to Queens for the groceries, and my meds have been delivered." Her frustration at the enforced inactivity showed in her voice, "I'm going stir crazy in this house!"

"Would you like to get out of the house?"

"Yes."

"How about a scenic ride?"

She stared at him with longing, "I'd kill to get out

of the house for an hour."

"No time like the present." He stood and walked into the kitchen, evidently to inform the family of his plan. When he returned, he simply picked her up, green wrap and all and headed down the stairs. Outside, it was evident he had planned this because the Cherokee was parked close to the back door. He gently placed her in the front seat and waited while she buckled up.

"Are you set?" Deke slid under the wheel and pulled sunglasses down over his eyes. He turned the key, and they cruised down the drive, past the Space Needle, around the Safeco Field, and onto the bridge for Mercer Island. He took the first exit on the island and circled it on the border road. Glimpses of impressive estates were hidden behind fences, and wonderful landscaping caught her eye time and again. He looped back up onto I-5, took the exit across the lake, and resumed speed on the freeway, this time heading for Kirkland. At Kirkland, he again exited and cruised up and down streets, through neighborhood parks, and along thoroughfares.

She felt herself relaxing, the tension from her enforced inactivity seeping from her body. Just before the freeway in Kirkland, he pulled into the XXX Drive In and ordered milkshakes for them. After approximately thirty minutes, she realized he was heading toward the freeway again, this time merging onto the floating bridge to take them back across into Seattle. A little more than an hour had passed before he brought them back to Queen Anne and slid up the driveway and circled to deposit her at the back steps. He cut the engine, and she turned her head to smile at him.

"Thank you so much. This helped so much with my fidgetiness."

He leaned across the seat, "Let's see if this helps

even more," and his lips closed on hers. She closed her eyes and leaned into his warmth. Long-dead emotions rose within her, and she wrapped her right hand around his neck and pulled him closer into the kiss.

When they pulled apart a few moments later, neither of them broke the silence. After a final hug, Deke pushed open his door, came around for her, and silently carried her into the house. No one was in the living room when he entered the apartment, and after depositing her back on the couch, he kissed her brow, said goodbye, and left. She sat silently contemplating what the kiss now meant to their relationship. Not knowing what was next, she was glad when Maddie entered and talk became general.

Chapter 20

Over the next several days, she spent mornings in the day care having special time with the kids, one-on-one. However, much to her disgust, she found that by noon, she was exhausted. Deke carried her back upstairs after lunch, and she would nap on the couch until dinner time.

About four p.m. on Friday, someone knocked on the apartment door then turned the knob and entered. Chloe looked up to see her dad standing in the doorway. "Dad!" She spread her arms wide, and he crossed the room and stooped to give her a hug.

"How are you feeling, honey?" his eyes scanned her face looking for evidence of mistreatment.

"I'm fine. Doing better every day." She relaxed in his warm embrace. Did anyone ever outgrow their dad's hugs? "Mom and Maddie have been heaven sent. There hasn't been even a hiccup in running the day care. They've even been able to keep a lid on Daniel."

"And I can hardly wait to meet Mr. Daniel," dad chuckled.

She smiled, "He's a sweetie, but it takes an eagle eye to forestall his enthusiastic plans. He'll probably run the world some day."

She shifted her head to look at him, "Why are you here? Not that I'm sad," she hastened to assure him, "but what brought you to Seattle?"

"Your mom," he lifted her feet, sat on the end of the couch, and placed them in his lap. "I missed her; the house was empty, and I decided I would come and visit for the weekend. Plus, it's your birthday, so Michael, Ryan, and I came for your party."

"What about Annabelle and Shelby? Why only the guys?" His words suddenly penetrated, "Party? What party? I'm too old to have a party."

"Tosh," her dad said, "you're never too old for a birthday party, Chloe. Annabelle and Shelby had a band concert and some school dance – Sadie Hawkins or something – so they asked to stay with friends."

She relaxed, "Well, Zach will be thrilled that Ryan came. So I'm very glad for him, and it's always good to see you and my favorite brother-in-law." She grinned, "I can't believe I forgot it was my birthday. I must be getting old."

Supper was noisy and fun. She had been a little surprised but glad that Deke joined them. He had obviously gone home and cleaned up because he was wearing old jeans, topsiders, and a deep green, long-sleeved shirt. She tried her hardest not to notice how gorgeous he looked.

She wasn't surprised that the family began telling stories. They had discovered how much Zach enjoyed hearing about his mom as a girl and pulled a new one out for his delight every time they got together.

"Remember how happy Chloe was to get a real baby?" Dad started.

Mom grinned, "She knew the real thing when she saw it. She handed me her baby doll and demanded to hold the real baby. I found her doll in the trash later and had to dig it out to keep for her."

"Then," Dad inserted, "we had to watch you like a hawk. The first day we brought Maddie home she cried, and when we walked in to check on her, we found you standing on a chair by the crib with her tucked under your arm, about to jump off the chair to 'bring the real baby' to us."

"I probably dropped her sometime when you weren't looking," Chloe said thoughtfully. "That would explain her problems." And Maddie bumped her shoulder in mock outrage while everyone laughed.

Mom and Maddie had fixed her favorite meal: fried chicken, mashed potatoes and gravy, and corn. Dessert was raspberry cheesecake. She had spent most of supper glancing at the stack of gifts on the kitchen cabinet, and when Maddie deposited a slice of raspberry cheesecake in front of her and led everyone in singing Happy Birthday, she urged, "Presents!"

She opened Zach's first. It was a rectangle, approximately 8 x 10 inches and when it was unwrapped she stared at it in silence, overcome by his thoughtfulness. "Do you like it?" his anxious voice roused her. It was a pine jewelry box, lined with green felt. "Deke helped me make it."

Her eyes met Deke's smiling ones, and she felt tears wells up at his thoughtfulness for her son. "It's beautiful," she whispered huskily. "I will treasure it forever. Thank you, son."

Uncomfortable with the emotions, he jabbed her hand with a second package. This one was much larger. And heavier. "Here's one from Deke, open it," he urged.

She tore off the wrapping and stunned, stared at a hot pink, metal tool box. Deke said, "I thought your own toolbox was warranted so you could fix everything that Daniel breaks," and the table erupted in laughter.

She flipped up the lid and admired the set of tools.

The handles on each were a soft marshmallow pink rubber. The trim was black metal. "I love it!" she enthused. "Thank you so much."

Her mom eyed it closely, "Where'd you get it?" she inquired of Deke, "I want a set just like it for myself."

Deke smiled, "That Komen's cancer foundation has everything you can think of; all of it in pink." He added anxiously, "I hope you like pink."

She smiled at him warmly, "I love pink, and I love my tools. It's a wonderful gift."

"One thing's for sure, Mom," Zach grinned, "you won't have to worry about me borrowing any of your tools." Everyone laughed again.

Zach interrupted the unexpected pool of silence that followed, "Okay, Mom's choice. It's your birthday; what game do you want to play?"

Deke eyed them closely. This was evidently a family ritual. He watched Chloe squint while she pondered the options. "I want," she finally announced, "to play poker."

"No-o-o-o," Zach crossed his fingers at her laughing.

Everyone else laughed too, and Grandpa reminded him, "It's birthday girl's choice. Poker it is."

Zach groaned, but got off the chair to head out of the kitchen. "I'll get the cards; someone else get the chips. But I'm warning you, it'll be the fastest game in history with Mom playing. She's a shark." He poked his head back into the doorway, "I told you, Mom, if we are really short of cash, all you have to do is take a trip to Las Vegas. You'll clean up."

Chloe shook her head, "That's what suckers

always think, Zach. I'm many things, but when it comes to money, I'm never a sucker." She opened one of the upper cabinets, gave a short jump, and snagged a package off the top shelf. Then she hobbled to the table and dumped in the middle, groaning and rubbing her back, "Won't do that again. I forgot I'm not one hundred percent well yet."

Deke stared at the package of candy, nonplussed, "Skittles? Okay, now we've got our snack, but where are the chips?"

She grinned as she seated herself again, "These are the chips. The orange are ones, the browns are fives, the reds are twenties, and the yellows are hundreds. You reach your hand into the bag without looking, count out fifty chips, and that's your swag for the game."

He eyed her, "Swag?" politely.

She grinned and nodded.

He gave up, "Okay, works for me."

Faith nodded, "Works for us too. It's the way I taught all my kids their colors, numbers, and sequence." She patted the deck fondly, "Poker's a great game." Deke smothered a grin.

The playing commenced, and Deke quickly found that Zach had not been kidding. Chloe's luck was phenomenal. At one point, as he was pondering his next move, he popped a Skittle into his mouth.

Maddie noticed, "If you eat your chips, you don't get replacements."

Chloe nodded, "That's another great thing about using Skittles for chips. When you're playing with kids they usually eat more than they win so the games are very short."

###

The time following the accident flew for Chloe. Her mom and Maddie stayed for two weeks, and then she resumed half days in the day care, with Maria, Mrs. Thompson, and Tasha logging in extra hours to make up for her absence. She had had to take care not to sit too long or do anything too energetic, like lift a child, but otherwise, she had managed. She'd been exhausted each night and had fallen in bed right after supper.

Twice, Deke brought supper and stayed to help Zach with his skateboard. She had gone to sleep hearing the sounds of their voices at the kitchen table as they discussed the merits of plywood versus fiberglass.

A few weeks later, Deke invited them over for a barbecue "to repay you for all the meals you've fed me." Zach had promptly accepted for both of them. Although it was full winter in Seattle and the November days inevitably brought rain, in the Northwest barbecuing was done year round.

She and Zach pulled up to Deke's house promptly at six. Zach bounded out of the car as soon as it stopped, but she paused in her seat to admire his home. It seemed odd—except for the one glimpse she had of it the night they picked up Woofer, this was her first time to visit, while Zach had been here several times. Even in the falling rain and early-evening darkness, she could see that it was a beautifully restored house. A front porch, deeply roofed to protect anyone enjoying one of three rocking chairs sitting there, spanned almost the length of the house.

Deke watched her from the door. At the entrance, he leaned down and kissed her warmly, aware of her flush because Zach observed them, "Want the nickel tour?" He inquired.

"Yes," she said, retrieving her breath. She raised her head to look around. He had kept the exterior true to the period, but he had gutted the first floor so that it was essentially a great room. "Deke, this is gorgeous."

"It took me almost five years to finish, because I had to work at it in my spare time. I lived in the shop for the first year, until the inspector granted me occupancy." He turned with her to survey the room, his eyes reflecting that he still took pleasure in viewing it.

He walked her past the mission-style dining room set into the state-of-the-art kitchen. It opened onto an outdoor, flagstone patio where she could see a barbecue sending up puffs of smoke. Back in the great room there was a soft corduroy couch and red upholstered chairs gathered around the fireplace in a conversation grouping.

Along the back wall rose the staircase, and while she hoped she'd see the second floor someday, she didn't feel right about asking. He simply took her hand and led her up the stairs. A central hallway bisected the upper floor, with three doors opening off it. The door on the left-hand side enclosed a master bedroom and bath, with a small sitting room in front of the fireplace. She didn't linger long—didn't even enter, just paused to view the masculine appointments from the doorway. Back on the right-hand side of the hallway, the first space was a home office, and he explained, "My business office is in the shop; this is just a space to park my personal bills and stuff." The remainder of that side was two smaller bedrooms with a connecting bath between.

Zach bounded up the stairs to show her where he had slept while she was in the hospital.

Standing in the doorway of one of the bedrooms, which was empty, Deke admitted, "I have made bed sets twice for these rooms, however, every time a customer comes along, likes it, and buys it. That's why Zach slept on a daybed."

Later, out on the patio, Deke and Zach lounged in chairs, waiting for the charcoals to die down. "What's that building for?" Zach pointed to the shop abutting the garage.

"That's my future." He took a drink of his cola while Zach digested the remark, "Wanna see it?"

"Yeah."

He called to Chloe, and single file, they trooped across the flagstone pavers that lead the way from the house to the out buildings. Inserting a key in the solid metal door, he swung it open and stepped aside for them to enter.

They both paused just inside, struck by what lay before them. They were standing in a genuine woodworking shop.

Behind them, his voice sounded far away, "Remodeling is my livelihood, but someday this dream will be my living."

"You make furniture," she was dumbfounded.

"Yes ma'am."

Two of the walls were covered in pegboard on which hung every imaginable woodworking implement. Chloe recognized chisels, knives, and sanders but had no idea the purpose of the majority of the other tools. Each tool hung within its outline traced on the board. Within easy reach of the work table were rubber mallets, rolls of tape, bottles of glue, and jars of stain. A deep sink fit the corner of the room, and an air compressor sat beside it.

There were graduated sizes of chisels, clamps, and handsaws. Down the center of the room, electric sanders, routers, and lathes were positioned; a network of bright yellow, flexible hoses ran from each and across the ceiling to collect the sawdust and store it in a bin against the wall. Multi-drawer cabinets held router heads by the dozens, each inserted in a special slot in the drawers. On the front of each drawer were drawings of the specific pieces inside.

"What is this?" she inquired placing her hand on a small cabinet. He showed her, stripping it down and demonstrating all of its details. Listening to him and watching how gently his hand lay on the wood, she smiled. This was where his passion lay; this was his calling. She hoped it would soon become his sole occupation.

She tuned back into his summation, "It's a lady's chest of drawers with a secret compartment."

That got Zach's attention. He came right over to examine the piece.

"I made it out of birds-eye birch; it has ebony pulls, and this," he opened the top doors, about one-third of the height of the piece, "has adjustable shelves for holding larger objects like a jewelry box." Below the doors were four drawers, the top two approximately four inches deep and the bottom two about seven inches deep. The cupboard and drawers equaled approximately sixteen inches, and with it resting on twelve-inch pencil-post legs, the overall height was just over four feet. It was clean and spare and exquisite.

"Where's the secret compartment?" Zach jutted his chin over Deke's shoulder.

"Well, now, if I told you it wouldn't be a secret would it?" he drawled, grinning at Zach's concentration.

"Come on, Deke, show me," Zach wheedled.

“See if you can find it,” Deke encouraged. He stood back and invited Zach’s inspection. “I’ll tell you it’s a drawer, and it’s approximately four inches by twenty inches. He smiled while Zach went over the piece multiple times until he admitted defeat. Deke reached down and pressed an unseen button behind one of the front legs. A shallow drawer, the width of the front of the piece popped out. “See,” he explained to Zach, “you can’t see it because its frontispiece is actually the decorative molding at the bottom of the cabinet.”

Fascinated by all the projects, finished and unfinished, Chloe continued to wander. On the fourth wall, the one by which they had entered, were more half-finished pieces of furniture. She recognized a blanket chest, a headboard, and a deacon’s bench. She reached out to touch the piece closest to her. The cherry wood of the headboard gleamed richly in the light of the room. It looked like it belonged in a museum. The pediments were richly detailed, their curves reminiscent of angel wings and the six-foot finials that framed either side were topped with intricately carved pineapples. Tracing her hand delicately over the carvings, she amended her first observation, “You are an artist.” Her head turned to meet Deke’s eyes.

He flushed as if her opinion mattered a great deal to him. “Thank you,” he said gruffly.

Zach darted from work station to work station, eagerly examining everything. “Do you have a website? I could make one for you. This stuff is really cool.”

Chloe couldn’t keep her hands off the pieces; they just begged to be touched. “Where did you learn this?”

“Woodworking classes in state school,” he shrugged. “They taught me the basics, and my own desire to create the pictures in my head taught me the rest.” He looked around, the pride and satisfaction in his glance an almost palpable thing, "I want to make one-of-a-kind, custom furniture."

"How far are you from your dream?"

"If business continues at its present rate, I am hoping to do this full-time in about a year."

They returned to the house, where Deke and Zach cooked the steaks, and Chloe set out the side dishes. They spent an enjoyable evening together, but Chloe was aware the entire time that this was a new Deke she hadn't known existed.

She had, despite her good intention, begun to allow herself to dream about the three of them becoming something permanent. Now she faced that it wasn't going to happen. Deke had other dreams and saddling him with a family would derail those dreams that he had worked toward so diligently. He was younger; he deserved his chance. She was already headed toward middle age with a half-grown son. They did not need to complicate his life.

###

Chloe found that Deke filled her thoughts more and more. And the more he was resident, the more irritated she became. She was a mature mother of a teenager, not some teenager herself. Besides, Deke was younger than she was and had never before married. He had his whole life of choices before him, while hers were curtailed by decisions she had made a decade or more ago. Not that she regretted any of them, because she didn't; it just underscored how unsuitable her attraction to him was.

Maddie wasn't any help. She had listened while Chloe confided trying to fight her attraction to Deke and her guilt at being attracted to any man.

"Chloe, we get so caught up in making sure we don't get snared by lust that we forget God is the one who created sex. And sexual attraction is a natural part of a man and woman's relationship. A believer's difference is that hopefully we know that the attraction isn't enough for a relationship; we have to have more, but the *ba-da-bing* is a good thing."

"Then why do I feel so guilty?"

"Because in your mind you're still married to Phillip and acknowledging an attraction to someone else would be wrong. You need to bury Phillip in your mind; even if this thing with Deke doesn't lead anywhere. It's time to move on honey."

As if she had opened a secret door, that night Chloe dreamed of Phillip. In her dream, she was once again sitting by his bed in the hospital and Phillip was talking to her, 'Chloe, when I'm gone, don't allow yourself to grow old alone. Zach needs a father and you need someone alongside you.' She woke up then with tears flowing down her cheeks. She lay quietly in the dark; recalling Phillip's words and whispered, "You were such a good man. I will always love you, but I think I am ready to move on." She cried for only a few more minutes, then aware that a great peace resided within her, turned over and went back to sleep.

###

After Deke packed up his tools to head home, he turned his head to eye Chloe standing in the doorway. She had seemed distracted all day, and it irritated him. She was the hardest woman to read. Finally, he broke the silence, "Are you free Friday night to go out to dinner?"

She turned to look at him. "You just fed Zach and me last night. Why would you want to take us out somewhere Friday?"

He snorted, "I don't want to take you and Zach out," he enunciated clearly. "I'm asking you out. On another date." He watched the flush rise in her cheeks and the hesitation in her eyes. He felt a surge of anger. "Come on Chloe, it cannot be a surprise that I'm attracted to you."

She was surprised, he could see that now. "I'm older than you," she blurted.

"So?"

She frowned, that hadn't been the deterrent she'd expected, "I have a teenage son."

"And?" He spoke impatiently, waiting for her to get to the point.

"Why?" She had run out of excuses.

"Why?" he thundered. "For heaven's sake, woman, isn't it obvious? I love you."

She gaped at him, and then as he watched, her eyes filled with tears and a smile equal to the sun breaking over clouds at dawn filled her face, "You love me?"

"Well, I intended to wait awhile and court you before blurting it out, but yes, I love you," he muttered.

She launched herself across the yard, and he caught her in his arms and kissed her.

Zach stumbled outside a moment later and saw his mom and Deke kissing, "Whoa!"

His response alerted Tasha, who poked her head out the door and squealed in delight. Her excitement brought Maria, and the sound of all three voices talking, brought Deke and Chloe back to the realization that they weren't alone.

Deke lifted his head, holding Chloe securely in his

grasp so she couldn't get away, as was telegraphed by the tenseness of her spine. "Do you mind? I'm trying to propose here." The ensuing chorus brought a grin to his face, while Chloe buried her face in his shoulder.

Epilogue
Two Years Later

Deke and Zach stood side-by-side outside the nursery window, both of them gazing at Baby Girl Hudson. All they could see was a pink bundle and the top of a pink knit cap. One itsy-bitsy fist propped atop the blanket opened into a tiny starfish then closed again.

Zach gave a deep sigh, "Boy! A girl. We're going to be busy watching that she doesn't get hurt."

Deke looped an arm around Zach's neck. He'd grown like a weed in the past year and begun to fill out. A ghost of a mustache filled his upper lip.

"A girl," he echoed, wondering if his heart would ever settle down again. "What do we know about raising girls?"

A clatter behind them made them turn to see the family tumbling through the door. Maddie and Faith were nose to nose for the lead, and he and Zach were enveloped in hugs and kisses.

"A girl!" Faith's light voice held a hint of tears. He hugged her warmly then grasped her shoulders and turned her toward the glass. "That's her, Baby Girl Hudson," he pointed proudly to the bassinette.

"Oh," she clasped her hands together and tears filled her eyes.

Deke caught Zach's eye and it was all either of them could do to hold back a laugh.

You would think he would have adjusted to new beginnings by now. That was all that the past couple of years had held for him. First Chloe and he had to learn to work as a couple. They both had realized there was a lot that needed to be settled between them before marrying. He had watched Chloe learn to accept him as a partner in raising Zach and Zach learn to accept another male authority in his life. It hadn't been easy, but the relationship he and Zach now had made it all worthwhile.

Second big adjustment was coming to an agreement about their businesses. He had been adamant that Chloe not give up her dream. He insisted that she could close the day care and open a bed-n-breakfast. She had been equally stubborn that it wasn't what she was going to do. "You are not going to give up your dream for us," her voice had been passionate.

"I figure I can go full-time within a year. I already have contracts with a couple of design studios downtown. So far my pieces have sold fairly quickly, and the people who have ordered custom pieces have been pleased. Personal recommendations are the very best. When people see a piece at a friend's home, and that friend recommends me whole-heartedly, it comes back to me in the way of additional business.

###

"Chloe, I'm not giving up my dream. I'm just setting the launch date back. I don't mind."

"Well, I do," her hair glowed and her eyes snapped. "You have worked hard for this chance.

"I do not have a career I dream of doing. I have totally different priorities in my life. I only wanted the bed-n-breakfast because it was a dream I shared with Phillip, something for our retirement. It was gone when he died. I do not want to run a day care either. I want to provide a home for you and Zach and any other children we may have and help you achieve your dream."

He got lightheaded for a moment, thinking about a tiny red-headed mini-Chloe staring back at her, hands on hips just like her mama. He could hardly wait to see those battles.

"You have worked too hard to build your furniture business. You have unbelievable talent. That is what we should be concentrating on."

They had gone for counseling with Pastor Markham and with his guiding wisdom, found that all obstacles were surmountable. He had agreed to attend a PAS, and Chloe had accompanied him. At the symbolic funeral ceremony on the final night, when he gave his unknown child an identity and released *Matthew* and his pain to God, he felt like a twenty-ton load of logs had rolled off his heart. He was finally free to walk in God's grace.

Almost six months to the date of their engagement, Deke received contracts for custom furniture from three design houses. It was enough promise for them to take the big step. She listed the day care. And no one was more surprised than she when Mrs. Thompson bought it.

She had cornered Chloe in her office the morning it appeared on the market to tell her. Chloe was shocked, "But you just retired, Mrs. Thompson. Are you sure?"

"Yes, I had enough of retirement in the six months before I came to work for you. But I know that my strength is in administration. You've got a good staff. If they'll remain with me, I definitely want to purchase it." So it had been done, and Maria and Tasha had been glad to remain.

They married on a beautiful June morning the following spring. What a ball that had been. The whole clan had gathered in her parents' backyard for a day-long party. Mrs. Watanabe had made the trip and to his surprise and delight, Dave and Bea Menodine had come. The day had begun at nine a.m. with a breakfast, followed by a simple marriage ceremony—Maddie had stood up with Chloe, and Zach had been his best man.

She and Zach had moved into Deke's immediately following their honeymoon, although the first month of their marriage Zach had spent in Yakima at Ryan's. Maddie had insisted, "You and Deke need time to yourselves. Let him stay with us. He loves it here, and he and Ryan will have a blast." And Deke and Chloe had admitted their month alone had been a wonderful time of settling, getting to know each other, and fun. However, they both admitted missing their kid.

She had taken over the books for Hudson Home Furnishings and had immediately begun to advertise his business. Building on his budding network, she had added enough clients within six months for him to quit worrying about being able to support his new family and to hire a full-time assistant. Zach was learning the trade and showing remarkable creative genius and spent as much time as possible with him in the shop.

The vibrancy of their lives sometimes made him wake up in a cold sweat for fear it had disappeared while he slept. Now, observing the family chattering excitedly about his daughter, hugging and laughing, he closed his eyes at the overwhelming thankfulness he had at the blessings God had given him. As Chloe had said, He was the God of second chances, and he was so blessed.

Questions for Discussion

1. Do you believe in love at first sight?
2. Have you ever heard of Post Abortion Syndrome? If you need more information go to: http://www.holyfamilycounseling.org/resources.html
3. Why do you believe Chloe had such a problem with her mother?
4. Should you be in the same situation as Chloe, would you have made different choices when your husband died?
5. Would you say that Deke's arrival into the lives of Zach and Chloe was a God orchestrated thing? Why or why not?
6. Have you gone through the loss of someone you loved? Did your personality change, and if so, how did it affect you and those around you?
7. Do you feel that Chloe fell in love with Deke partly to provide Zach a father? Is that wrong?
8. Do you feel Deke's assessment that Zach was abusing Chloe correct?
9. Have you found yourself, like Chloe, believing you had all the answers and needed no help?
10. Which relationship in the book touched you the most? Deke and Zach? Deke and Mrs. Watanabe? Chloe and Maddie?

Made in the USA
Las Vegas, NV
03 December 2021